Ava had to go now, before she lost her nerve.

She stuffed the letter in an envelope, scribbled his name on it, checked the window facing Zach's one more time and sneaked quietly out her front door, stepping carefully to make as little noise on the gravel as possible.

She reminded herself to breathe as she moved. That was the thing about sneaking...your instinct was to hold your breath, which was, of course, the worst thing a person could do when trying to be quiet. Finally, she made it, pulling the mailbox open slowly. It squeaked a little but she slipped the metal flap shut and turned back toward her house.

A few more steps and she'd be home free.

Which was precisely when the door to Zach's house burst open and Zach came flying down the stairs, a look of pure panic on his face.

"Zach?" she said, and as he ran toward her, the terrible empty feeling of having to leave morphed into something else. Something along the lines of nauseated terror. "What's wrong?"

"She's gone," he said, out of breath, jumpy and on the verge of tears. "Chloe is gone."

Dear Reader,

I can't wait for you to meet Ava and Zach, a sunshine/grumpy pairing if there ever was one. But truth be told, Ava's sunny nature and her appreciation for life is new, born out of dark secrets in a past she was lucky to escape. And even though Zach has little patience for the tourists who flood to town during the annual Apple Cider Festival, he will always be one of those guys who will do anything for anyone, even if he throws out a few complaints while he's at it.

When Ava's past comes back to haunt her, everyone in town is put in danger, and Ava and Zach have to work together to set everything right again...all while navigating new layers of a relationship that has always been firmly planted in the friend zone.

Fun fact: *A Spy's Secret* is my first story set in the quaint fictional town of Ambrosia Falls. I have so many ideas for this little town (and even a couple outlines already written) and hope someday I'll get to tell all the stories from this charming place filled with lovable and quirky characters.

Thank you so much for reading!

Rachel

A SPY'S SECRET

RACHEL ASTOR

ROMANTIC SUSPENSE

Harlequin®
ROMANTIC SUSPENSE™

Recycling programs for this product may not exist in your area.

ISBN-13: 978-1-335-50252-0

A Spy's Secret

Harlequin Enterprises ULC
22 Adelaide St. West, 41st Floor
Toronto, Ontario M5H 4E3, Canada
www.Harlequin.com

Printed in Lithuania

MIX
Paper | Supporting responsible forestry
FSC® C021394

Rachel Astor is equal parts country girl and city dweller who spends an alarming amount of time correcting the word *the*. Rachel has had a lot of jobs (bookseller, real estate agent, 834 assorted admin roles), but none as, *ahem*, interesting as when she waitressed at a bar named after a dog. She is now a *USA TODAY* bestselling author who splits her time between the city, the lake and as many made-up worlds as possible.

Books by Rachel Astor

Harlequin Romantic Suspense

The Suspect Next Door
Undercover Heist
A Spy's Secret

Visit the Author Profile page at Harlequin.com

Prologue

Something had been off with Justin for weeks.

The change was subtle—most people would never notice—but the Sparrow's training taught her to spot inconsistencies. She couldn't pinpoint what it was, exactly, but he was acting strange. And when he kissed her goodbye that fateful Tuesday morning, a thought hit her like a truck, filled to the brim with trepidation.

Oh God, he's going to ask me to marry him.

Was that even something she wanted?

Judging from the way her stomach flopped when the thought crashed through her brain, it wasn't. Except, Justin was the best guy she knew. She only trusted two people in the world, and he was one of them.

In their business—a business literally built on lies—trust was in short supply, only coming after years of earning it. And Justin had earned it. He'd been her partner for four years before they ever got romantically involved. It was inevitable the relationship would eventually turn into something more.

But they'd only been a couple for eight months.

Of course, time acted differently when you were in the spy business. Forced to depend on someone to keep you safe when they held your life in their hands made everything more intense, heightened. And as her communications tech for years, he'd kept her safe through inconceivable danger.

Lately though, things were less…exciting. Which of course had been inevitable too.

Maybe she was reading too much into things. They'd only been living together a few months, after all. And even that had been more out of convenience when the lease came up on his apartment. She owned this huge, beautiful place with plenty of space, and it seemed like the logical thing to do. But now that the thought had entered her brain, she needed to know.

Justin wouldn't be back for hours.

So she began to search.

Thoughts jolted through her. Thoughts like *too soon*, *bad timing* and…*I have to get out.*

Sparrow's training taught her how to conduct a thorough search while making sure to keep everything intact. Neat. No suspicion aroused.

She came up empty in the house. Deep down she suspected she would. If a ring existed, she knew where it would be.

The shed.

Justin had the small building delivered when he moved in.

"I could never do this stuff in my old apartment, but I've wanted this for years," he'd said.

And it didn't matter to Sparrow. Her property had plenty of space, tucked out of the way from prying eyes, far away from the city. She loved being lost in the desert. And so, the shed was installed. A dark room for his photography. No matter how advanced technology got, Justin swore something about film was truer, more real. There was an art to it.

Sparrow thought his passion was endearing.

What would she do if she found a ring? Make hints that it was too soon? But how could she possibly do that without rousing his suspicions that she'd discovered it? Justin was trained to spot lies too.

Sparrow flung the shed door open and flicked on the light. Everything appeared in order. *Exacting* order. One more thing that differed between the two of them. Sparrow wasn't messy, but she wasn't anal either. Working undercover meant blending in, and she always thought Justin's obsessive neatness was too over-the-top to blend. But no one would ever discover his perfectionism way out here, so she let it go. Although, when she routinely found her toiletry bottles lined up with the labels all facing front and in order from shortest to tallest, she always wanted to mix them all up into a disorganized group. One time, she did exactly that. He'd come up behind her, grasping her in a tight hug, as if he was physically trying to stop her. "I love that you love a little chaos," he'd said.

"It's hardly chaos," Sparrow replied, pulling gently out of his grasp.

The bottles were once again lined in military precision the next time she came into the room.

The urge now to mix up the shelves of chemicals, film and tools was immense, but she was far too professional. Start at one end and be methodical. Leave no stone—or bottle—unturned.

I have to get out.

Stop, she told herself. *Things are fine. Why do you always search for trouble whenever things are going well?*

Unfortunately, she knew the answer. Because she always found trouble. And when she tipped over a black plastic chemical jug in the middle of ten other black plastic chemical jugs, hearing a telltale click of a door unlatching, she realized she'd found it once again.

For a second, she actually wished she'd discovered what she'd gone looking for. She'd realized in the past few minutes, with absolute clarity, she did not want to marry this man, but still, a ring would have been so much better than this.

Sparrow shot off a quick text before she pulled the trapdoor, which had unlatched from the floor when she tilted the bottle. Annoyance rolled through her. The bastard did this on her own property right under her nose, probably during the Marseille job when he claimed he was sick. She should have caught it. She'd been trained to catch things like this. Trained not to trust anyone. But she did. She trusted Justin. Sure, he had his idiosyncrasies, but this was Justin.

I have to get out.

Sparrow grabbed for her gun, but it wasn't there. Of course it wasn't. All her weapons were in the house. But she couldn't turn back. Irritation and curiosity fueled her forward.

Until a moment ago she believed she had control. Of her life, her career, of everything. But suddenly nothing was true anymore. And with the passion of a thousand sports fans whose team had just lost, she hated that she'd been played.

The bunker was pitch-black. She lit the screen on her

phone to search for a switch, but there was only a simple light bulb with a string. She pulled it, sucking in a breath, bracing herself for anything.

Still, she was not prepared for what she saw.

Surveillance.

A typical spread. Photos of the target. Maps of where they'd been. Movements tracked down to the minute. Schedules.

But it was the face of the target, staring back from all those photos, that almost broke her.

Her face.

Some of the pictures were from before she'd even met Justin. Years before. Of her shopping, eating…sleeping. Newspaper articles from when her parents were killed ten years ago. Family history. Not that there was anyone left anymore.

The pictures and articles grew older as she moved down the wall.

She reached up to pull the string on the second light above her.

Click.

No light came on. In an instant she understood her fatal mistake. A barely audible squeal pierced her ears. And then the blast.

Blinding, deafening, jolting her forward. Backward? She didn't know.

Pain.

And as the world began to go black, Sparrow had only one thought left.

I have to get out.

Chapter 1

Five years later...

Zach was annoyed. This time of year was always so...
much. Everyone in town seemed to think the annual
Apple Cider Festival was the best thing ever, and sure,
most of the people in town made half their year's sal-
ary during the week as several thousand people from all
over the state and beyond flocked to town, so he could
kind of understand, but man, all these tourists were just
so...touristy.

The bell above the coffee shop door chimed, his
shoulders rising further toward his ears. It was the third
time in the last five minutes he'd heard its tinkling ring,
messing with his focus.

"Oh my gawd, this place is so stinking cuuuuute,"
the woman who'd entered said.

Zach closed his eyes and pulled a long breath in
through his nose. *Breathe*, he tried to encourage himself, *just breathe*.

"Welcome to The Other Apple Store," Ava said from
behind the counter.

Somehow, she actually seemed to enjoy when these
people barged into her life and her store. Of course she

did—that was Ava Katz. Good with everybody. Always kind. Always patient. Although she'd only been in town for five years, and he'd been here his whole life, so maybe the novelty hadn't worn off for her yet.

The woman whose jangle interrupted Zach turned to her friend, gasping with excitement fit for a teen pop concert. "Did you hear that? The Other Apple Store! Like the computer one except, like, this one actually sells real apple stuff."

"I know!" her counterpart squealed.

They erupted into a shriek slash giggle slash "oh my gawd" fest. And Zach just knew they'd gone shopping for their Apple Cider Festival uniforms of cable knit sweaters, boots with wool socks peeking out and winter hats with giant pom-poms at some overpriced hipster store too. A small growling groan escaped him before he could catch it.

Ava beamed while Zach tried not to say anything more under his breath. She caught his eye and pumped her eyebrows at him like she was having the time of her life.

Which, knowing Ava, she probably was.

It was one of the things he loved most about her—she seemed to find genuine enjoyment in almost anything.

He shook the thought from his head, reminding himself he wasn't supposed to love anything about Ava. She was off limits—too important a friend—a friendship he couldn't risk with silly, romantic notions.

Maybe if he'd made a move in those first months after she'd arrived in town…but that time was long gone. He remembered the first time he saw Ava, laughing and joking with the movers like she'd known them all her life.

She'd stopped him in his tracks.

She was beautiful, but it wasn't just the way she looked. There was something about the way she treated the movers. Like kindness was her religion.

But Chloe had been his focus, only five back then, and time for romance didn't exist. Now, all these years later, Ava and Zach had both put each other so wholly in the friend zone it was far too late for anything else. Besides, he'd learned that lesson with Kimberly. Never date a friend. There was too much to lose.

And he honestly didn't know who he'd be anymore without Ava's friendship.

It was too important.

She was too important.

Another flurry of giggles shocked him out of his thoughts, the ladies trying—and failing—to pick something out at the bakery counter.

"Everything looks so goooooood," one of them said.

Zach couldn't stop his eyes from rolling. They weren't wrong, but why did they have to be so loud and all "Look at me! Look at me!" about everything? But Ava never lost her hundred-watt smile, her patience rivaling that of a saint. She shot him a quick wink, which reminded him he didn't have to be such an old curmudgeon about the festival, but honestly, these people were a nightmare to deal with. He thanked his lucky stars he didn't have to work part-time in the gift shop anymore like he did in high school. Talk about a horror show.

"Apple Fritter, Caramel Apple Cake, Apple Spiced Cookies. You sure do have a lot of apple stuff," the second tourist said.

"Well," Ava replied, still genuinely charmed by the

women, "it is the Apple Cider Festival after all." Her smile grew even wider, and her eyes sparkled.

"Oh my gawd, you're right!" the first woman squealed. She jump-turned toward her friend and gasped. "I just had the *best* idea. We should buy one of everything!"

Her friend's eyes went wide as if the woman had discovered gold or cured cancer or something. She began to nod vigorously. "We totally should! We are here all weekend, after all!"

Ava packed up their enormous order and sent them on their way with complimentary cups of apple cider you would have thought were filled with diamonds the way they'd reacted.

"This town is so friendly! No wonder Trixie and Alistair recommended this place so highly."

Zach had never been so happy to hear the little bell over the door as he watched them walk out. The sigh he let out might have been a bit more audible than he'd intended.

"You okay there, Zach?" Ava called from behind the counter.

He looked at her, more serious than he'd ever been. "I honestly don't know how you do it."

She shrugged. "I'll never get sick of this. All the people, the energy, the excitement…the apples," she said. He didn't know how she could routinely make her eyes twinkle the way they did, like a kid on Christmas morning. "And speaking of apples," she continued, sneaking into the kitchen and returning with a plate covered in a napkin. "I present to you—" she paused both for effect and to fling off the napkin with a flourish "—the Apple Butter Glazed Spiced Pecan Blondie!"

He stared at her, expressionless. "The name's a bit of a mouthful, isn't it?"

But Ava simply grinned. "Not as much of a mouthful as you're about to have," she said, grabbing the fork off his plate and shoving a bite into his mouth before he could say another word.

And of course, the dessert was perfection. Like everything she baked. As he chewed the buttery, sweet goodness, he couldn't help but wonder how he'd gotten so lucky as to be her resident taste-tester.

"That is good," he said, "really good. But how come you're always trying your new stuff out on me?"

"Ah, there are two reasons," Ava said. "First, you're always here."

He tilted his head in agreement. He basically considered The Other Apple Store his unofficial coworking space.

"And second," she continued, her smile widening, "if even you, Old Mr. Grumpy Pants, like something, I know I've got a winner."

And as Zach's eyes rolled so hard he nearly saw his brain, hers sparkled brighter than ever.

Honestly, Ava loved how grumpy Zach was. Like her very own little Grumpy Cat in human form. He came off unbearably gruff to new people, but once you got to know him, everybody loved him—even his grumpy ways. Especially his grumpy ways. Because he was the most generous, empathetic, helpful old grump anyone could be lucky enough to know.

"Besides, you were the first person to welcome me

to Ambrosia Falls, so I guess I have a soft spot for ya," she said, shoving his shoulder a little.

He smiled.

She remembered the first time she'd seen that smile. Her first day in town had been a long one…after an even longer month. She'd been holed up in the safe house all alone—not supposed to even glance outside, though she obviously took a peek once in a while. A person isn't meant to not see the outdoors, to not get a glimpse of sunshine.

She didn't get much of a say in what her house would be like—she couldn't exactly leave protection to go house shopping, but she did get to pick out her furniture—thank you online shopping! She could only hope everything would go with whatever house she landed in. Ava purposely picked things different from her old place, which had been minimalist, stark and modern, and thank goodness she did. The giant old Eaton farmhouse would have looked ridiculous decked out like that. But she'd chosen comfortable and cozy things, and after a bustling day of movers and unpacking, things felt more settled.

But it had been so…quiet.

Alone again, Ava thought. Hadn't she always known she was destined to live like this? To always be on the outside looking in? Why would a new town be any different? Except she was out now. She wasn't a spy anymore. She wasn't Sparrow. Relief and a little sadness washed over her. For a while she had loved that life. The excitement, the danger…but it got old faster than she had thought.

In theory Ava didn't have to worry about letting people get close anymore. That version of her disappeared off the face of the earth, replaced by this new "normal" person.

But what did that even mean?

And then Zach showed up at her door with a welcome to the neighborhood gift, a six-pack of beer. The night had been so hot the flyaway tendrils that had escaped Ava's ponytail stuck to the back of her neck as she opened the door and got her first glimpse of the man who would become so important to her.

"Hey," he'd said and introduced himself. "This, uh… this was all I had." He lifted the six-pack, looking a little sheepish. "I wanted to bring a bottle of wine or something, but the store was closed and I figured it was better than nothing…"

"It's perfect," Ava said, charmed by the way his words trailed off and he rubbed the back of his neck, clearly uncomfortable. But with the impeccable manners of someone raised in a small town where community meant everything, he couldn't leave a new neighbor waiting without something to welcome them home.

Little did he know how perfect the gift really was, at the perfect time in the perfect little town.

They didn't chat much that night, but his smile, along with the beer, did make her feel welcome. She'd been so terrified normal wasn't possible, yet here she was, normal flourishing all around her.

The bells chimed above the door again, and Zach's face grimaced automatically, but when he saw who entered, his expression quickly changed.

Only one person could put a smile on his face like that. Sadly, it wasn't her, Ava thought.

"Hey, Chloe," she said, not having to turn to know who'd come in.

"Hey, Ava," came the adorable chirp of a voice. "How is your day going?"

Ava turned and smiled. Chloe had to be the most adorable kid ever. Ten going on thirty, she loved to spend time at the coffee shop, preferring grown-up conversations to the ones with her friends. What kind of kid asks the adults in their life how their day is going before the adults get the chance to ask first?

"Even better now that you're here, kid," Ava said, then gave Chloe a sideways, mischievous look. "Got a new one for ya." She held the blondie plate out and grabbed a clean fork off the counter.

Chloe's eyes got wide as she slipped into the booth opposite her dad. "A new one?"

Ava nodded, opening her mouth to speak, but Zach interrupted her.

"Don't ask her what it's called unless you have until next Monday for her to tell you. Just eat it, trust me."

Chloe laughed and nodded, knowing full well how Ava liked to name her recipes after the long list of ingredients. "Don't worry, we'll come up with something amazing."

"I'm counting on it, kid," Ava said, glancing up out the window.

She loved this time of year. The festival helped stoke a tiny longing for something else in her life—something a bit more exciting. She loved this new life, but it was so very opposite of how her world used to be. And sure, a small-town fruit festival wasn't exactly the epitome of intrigue, but the whole town came to life with activity, and that was good enough to quell the yearning.

But as she took in the view of Ambrosia Falls—the glorious colors on the autumn trees, the ever-growing groups of tourists, everybody working hard to erect temporary tents and booths—something seemed…off.

She crossed her arms and tilted her head, trying to figure out what bothered her.

She moved slowly away from Zach and Chloe, toward the door, opening it slowly, the gears of her mind cranking.

The seasonal water tower. Was it…swaying?

Ava glanced at the trees surrounding the town and while a few leaves fluttered gently in the light breeze, it certainly wasn't enough to make the enormous makeshift water tower—filled only once a year to cover the needs of the town as the population quadrupled in size—sway.

And then she heard the groan.

Ava's eyes darted to the tents and cloth-roofed booths near the bottom of the tower.

"Move!" she yelled at the top of her lungs, her feet already in motion.

People turned to see what the commotion was about, but not a single soul appeared the least bit alarmed. "Move!" she screamed again, realizing Annie's booth—the one filled with a year's worth of crocheted sweaters, both for people and pets, as well as hats and baby booties—stood directly under the tower.

The tower began to tilt.

Ava kept screaming, "Move! The tower! Move!" as a few people started to figure out what was going on, their eyes nearly popping out of their heads before they turned to flee.

Annie would never be able to get out of harm's way

in time. She didn't have the best hearing, and the fact she needed a walker definitely wouldn't help.

The sound of wood splintering must have finally reached Annie. She began to turn, trying to see what was going on behind her, but there was no time.

Ava dove at her, circling her arm under Annie's the way one might saving a drowning victim and pulling her as far away from the inevitable disaster as she could, hoping she wouldn't do any physical damage to the poor woman.

The sound of the crash brought with it a flashback of the fateful night back at the desert bunker when Ava's whole world imploded, both literally and figuratively. Screams erupted as water exploded from the enormous plastic tank, drowning the street, the booths, and soaking all of the people standing nearby.

An explosive squawking came from Miss Clara's booth as her prize rooster, Captain Applebottom—the fair's unofficial mascot for the past three years running—was hit with the surge. Feathers and water flung from the cage violently before Miss Clara rushed to soothe the poor creature who was somehow, miraculously, still clucking.

When the water finally settled, flowing rapidly over Ava's feet and into the sewer grates on the edges of Main Street, Annie turned to Ava, blinking. "Are you alright, dear?" she asked, calm as could be.

Ava nodded, although she felt more than a little bit away from alright. "Yeah," she said, still panting. "Yeah, I'm alright. Are you?"

Annie looked down at herself as if checking to make sure. "Yes, yes, I think so, dear. Thank you for saving me."

Ava gave the woman a hug—more for her own benefit than Annie's—and said, "Yeah, of course. Anytime."

"Ava!" Zach's terrified scream rose above the rest.

She turned as Zach rushed up to her, putting his hands on her shoulders and surveying her head to toe. "What the hell were you thinking, running in like that?"

"Well." Annie's reply came quicker than Ava could form words. She always had that trouble whenever Zach touched her, no matter how innocent it was. "She was saving my life, of course," Annie said, as if delivering any old sentence.

Ava supposed poor Annie was a bit in shock, looking at her booth. The creations she'd taken all year to make with love and craftsmanship had become flattened mats of soggy yarn, floating pitifully in the muddy water.

"I wonder how on earth something like this could have happened," Annie said, expressing the words everyone was thinking.

Chapter 2

Zach was more than a little relieved everyone appeared okay as he tried to process the situation. Ava had just… taken off. Dove headfirst into danger. He thought he knew her pretty well, had spent nearly every day of the past five years with her, but he honestly would have pegged her as a flight-er, not a fighter.

He was also embarrassed to admit he was more than a little turned on by her bravery and, holy mother-of-pearl, the way she looked with her clothes soaked and clinging to every inch of her. He shoved those thoughts as deep and as far into the corner of his mind as possible.

He still held Ava's shoulders, double- and triple-checking that she was all in one piece. One nonsmashed piece. The water tower had come so close. From his angle he swore it came straight down on them. Right on top of poor Annie and… Ava.

What if something had happened to her? The thought made him instantly sick, and that realization made him even sicker. He'd been working so hard to keep her at arm's length, to center himself solidly in the friend zone.

He lowered his arms and took a sheepish step back, clearing his throat.

"We need to figure out what happened here," Barney from the candle stand said. "Do you think this was an accident?"

For the first time, Zach considered the possibility it might not be.

"Of course it was an accident, you fool," said Miss Clara, the one person in town you could count on to always give Barney a hard time.

"You know, Clara, contrary to your belief, there are things in this world even you don't know every answer to," Barney said. Unfortunately, you could always count on Barney to volley that hard time right back.

The two started bickering like they were in grade school, the volume rising quickly. Others tried to jump in and calm them down, but Zach had watched the scene play out a hundred times before, and it would never work. He raised his hands to his mouth and let out a deafening whistle, quickly regretting it when every eye in town turned toward him.

"Look, none of us knows what happened here. Maybe instead of arguing all day, we could, I don't know, examine the tower and see if we can figure it out?" He glanced from one person to the next to the next, but not a single one backed him up.

Until he locked eyes with Ava. "Sounds reasonable," she said, her breath surprisingly back to normal already, not at all like she'd recently dead-sprinted to save a friend. Suddenly, everyone standing on the street agreed. Zach tried not to take it personally that he'd lived in Ambrosia Falls his entire life, was related to some of these people, yet the moment Ava opened her mouth, they hung on her every word.

Not that he could blame them.

"Well, you guys take care of it then," Barney said, apparently all too happy to spout on about needing to figure everything out, but not too keen on actually doing it.

"Um, who's taking care of it?" Ava asked.

"You two," he said, vaguely waving toward Zach and Ava.

"Makes sense to me," Miss Clara said. "You're the mystery expert, after all."

Zach closed his eyes. "Seriously? The first time in the history of the world you two agree on something, and that something is to send a mystery writer off to solve a real mystery?"

"Sure," Barney said, without a hint of irony.

Zach opened his mouth to argue, but the crowd had already started dispersing, beginning the cleanup before more tourists could arrive.

Ava put her hand on his shoulder. Her touch sent an all-too-familiar jolt through him. "It's fine," she said. "Maybe the whole thing was engineered poorly or something. I mean, a giant tub of water on those spindly wooden legs. This was bound to happen at some point."

"Shouldn't we call the authorities or something?"

Ava shrugged. "I guess if we find something suspicious, but you know as well as I do that unless something catastrophic happens, we're so far out in the middle of nowhere we don't hit anyone's radar."

He let out a long, slow breath. "Yeah," he said, remembering the time Hanson's horse got stolen. The law took six days to come out to investigate, and even then, it was a reserve officer who'd come...one Hanson suspected was sent due to some kind of a hazing situation.

"Honestly, I think we're about as good a choice as any," Ava said. "At least we'll keep it together. Imagine some of the conspiracy theories Jackson or Mae might come up with?" she asked, the spark back in her eyes.

Zach sighed. "Fine, let's get this over with."

They made their way through the rubble, mud and flurry of townsfolk cleaning up with no regard for the fact they might be ruining evidence. They eventually got to the area where the wooden stumps of the base were still sticking out of the ground, the wood splintered and shattered.

"Doesn't look like the legs were cut or anything," Zach said, easily pulling a sharp piece of wood from the jagged stump.

"Termites?" Ava asked.

"I don't know. Might be rot, but either way this doesn't look like anything too nefarious, other than an incredible lack of safety inspection."

Ava nodded. "Well, case closed, I guess. Come on, I'll buy you a beer for the good work. I feel like we both deserve one."

"Yeah." Zach watched as Ava moved back toward the coffee shop, tucking a piece of wet hair behind her ear as she carefully picked her way through the wreckage.

But something still felt off about the whole thing. The water tower was quite literally on its last legs, but still. Why today? The wind wasn't blowing that hard. And what were the chances the tower would fall in the exact direction to put people in harm's way?

He shook his head and threw the splinter to the ground.

Perhaps he wasn't the best person to do any investigating. His writer's imagination definitely got the best of him sometimes.

* * *

Ava watched as the last of the vendors closed up their booths for the night. The rest of the afternoon had gone by in a blur of mud and tourists and baked goods. Zach had been surprisingly focused after the incident, incredibly productive over in his corner frantically typing the afternoon away.

She flipped the sign on the door to Closed, then finally cracked the beer she had promised Zach and set it on his table. She cracked another for herself and slipped into the booth opposite him.

"Well, that was a day," she said.

He slid his laptop aside and pulled the beer toward him. "Definitely something."

Ava took a swig. "Looks like the excitement gave you a shot of inspiration though," she said, motioning to his laptop.

"Yeah, I guess so. Powered through a chapter and a half."

Ava raised her eyebrows. "Nice."

They talked about what happened, then a bit about the festival, and went on to everything else under the sun. Chloe's grandma was with her for the evening, so Zach was in no hurry.

Funny, no matter how much time they spent together, they never ran out of things to say.

But Ava always wondered about one thing, and with three beers behind her, she found the courage to bring up the subject that had been on her mind for years.

"You've never told me what happened with Chloe's mom." She held her breath.

For as long as she'd known Zach, he had been single, and she was more than a little curious why. Then again, she supposed she hadn't been involved with anyone either.

She expected him to wave her off, but to her surprise, he let out a breath and began to speak.

"I thought we wanted the same things. Kimberly was a little hard to please, but I felt like I pulled it off, at least at first. My debut book had been moderately successful, and some real money started to come in, so we were living the dream, I guess," he said, shrugging.

Ava nodded, not wanting to say anything, scared to break the spell.

"We'd been best friends ever since we were kids. She lived down the street, and we'd known each other since before we started grade school. Then when we did go to school, we kept being best friends. We depended on each other for everything."

"Sounds perfect," Ava said, nodding for him to continue.

"It was…mostly. She was adventurous, you know? And I was too for a while. After graduation we went on all these trips…white-water rafting, mountain excursions, zip lining, that sort of stuff. Life was fun, don't get me wrong, but I always felt like I was playing a part. Like it wasn't really *my* life."

Ava could relate so much more than he would ever know.

"She liked the lifestyle more than I did, but we were best friends, and making her happy made me happy." Zach squirmed in his seat a little.

"You know, for someone who makes their living as

a storyteller, you don't seem to be all that comfortable when you're telling one out loud."

He grinned. "That's the beauty of the computer. No one to judge until you know you've got it right. I can make as many changes as I want until I'm satisfied."

Ava's neck went hot, trying not to think about what Zach would look like satisfied. She cleared her throat. "I'm not judging you, Zach."

He nodded. "Yeah, I know." He took a long swig of his beer.

"So you were living the dream. What happened?"

Zach tilted his head. "I don't know exactly. I mean, we never discussed having kids, but I assumed, like a fool, I guess, that we both wanted the same things. She got pregnant and, well, it spooked her. She wasn't sure if she wanted a baby, but me," he said, staring off, a grin— elated, but somehow with a sadness to it too—spread across his face, "after knowing a part of me was growing into a tiny human, I couldn't think about anything else. I thought I wanted this life of adventure and travel and freedom, but the second even the *idea* of a kid entered the picture, I became obsessed."

Ava smiled. "Sounds about right."

He nodded. "It's who I am now, but I was a different person back then. I was scared too, but I convinced her to have the baby. And Chloe came along, and we tried for a while, Kimberly tried for a while, but motherhood didn't come naturally. She said she was never meant to be a mom and she left."

"I can't imagine how someone could leave their child."

Zach shrugged. "She was never cut out for it. I suppose I shouldn't have pushed, but I wanted to be a parent so badly. And Kim tries. I mean, she's a parental disaster, but she sends Chloe letters and presents and tries to stop in once in a while, but for the most part, Chloe and I are on our own."

Ava felt a squeeze in her heart. This man she admired so much—tried so hard *not* to admire as much as she did—had done such an amazing job raising a great kid all by himself. "Must have been hard on you all these years."

"The dad part hasn't been hard at all. I feel like you just love your kid and try to make good choices and do your best. The hardest part was losing my best friend, you know?"

Ava didn't know. She couldn't remember ever having a best friend, but she nodded anyway. "I'm sorry. It's hard to lose people." That she did know.

Zach nodded, drifting in his own thoughts. "Maybe Kimberly and I were never meant to be romantically involved. We probably should have stuck with being friends. Everything got screwed up once we became a couple."

Ava nodded. "There's always the chance you're going to lose the friendship if things don't work out."

"Exactly," Zach said. "But I did get the most important thing in my life out of the deal, so I suppose it was meant to be."

Ava smiled. Nodded. *Meant to be.* How nice to live a life where you could believe in "meant to be" and "happily-ever-after and all those fairy-tale notions.

"Well, I guess I better leave you to it," Zach said, probably realizing she still had a lot of cleaning up to do before returning at dawn to start tomorrow's baking.

And the day's baking would be intense. Two assistants were coming in at 5:00 a.m. in order to keep up with the demand.

"Thanks for the beer," he said, packing up his computer.

"And thanks for the story," she said. "I thought I knew almost everything about you, but I guess there's always more to learn."

She hated all the secrets she would never be able to tell him.

As Zach stood to leave, a frantic knock sounded at the door.

Zach sighed. "What now?"

Ava shot him a twinkling smile and went to unlock the door. Miss Clara burst through, nearly knocking her over.

"Miss Clara, what is it? Are you okay?" Zach asked.

"No! No, I'm not okay. You guys…" she said, trying to catch her breath, clearly beside herself. "Captain Applebottom is missing!"

Chapter 3

"This can't be a coincidence," Miss Clara said, looking around as if she might find Captain Applebottom right there in the room.

"A coincidence with what?" Zach asked.

"The water tower, of course," Miss Clara said, though Zach couldn't, for the life of him, figure out what one could possibly have to do with the other. "This has to be the work of those Pieville hooligans."

Zach nearly spit out a laugh trying to imagine the charming older ladies of Pieville creeping around town all dressed up in "hooligan" outfits, which, in his mind, consisted of head-to-toe black, perhaps with those eye masks that tied in the back of their various gray/purple/blue and heavily permed hairstyles. But he couldn't even get a snort out before Miss Clara went on.

"Everybody knows they've been trying for years to take over the festival scene around these parts—I mean, they changed the name of their entire town just to wrangle a few tourists—but if they think they can beat our cozy charm and friendly atmosphere, they have another thing coming."

"Friendly atmosphere. Right," Zach said, risking a

glance at Ava, who looked like she was enjoying every second of Miss Clara's rant.

He couldn't understand how Ava never seemed to tire of the ridiculous, and endless, "emergencies" the people of this town overreacted to on the daily. Or how she seemed to be enchanted by it instead of the correct reaction, which was, of course, exasperation.

"I'm sure Captain Applebottom is fine," he said in his most soothing voice.

Ugh, he hated saying the name of that damned chicken. The bird itself was okay, and he got that it was an homage to the Apple Cider Festival, but why did Miss Clara have to go and name him something so embarrassing to say out loud?

"Fine?" Miss Clara said, her voice screeching a bit. "Fine? That poor creature experienced the shock of his lifetime when the water tower came down this morning, and on top of that, now he's been abducted! How could you possibly say you're sure he's fine?" She broke off, pacing and muttering something under her breath that sounded a bit like, "Don't these people have any idea how important my sweet boy is to this town?"

"But we checked the tower, Miss Clara. You know we didn't find any signs of foul play," Zach said.

Miss Clara stopped her pacing to squint at Zach in a way that revealed how little she thought of his detective skills. "Yes, maybe the wood was rotting a little on the tower, but that does not mean there was no foul play! Anyone could have pushed it over."

Zach tried to picture what that would entail, but came up a bit short. To even think of standing under something, with all that weight teetering above—knowing the structure was so rickety it could simply be pushed over—a person would have to be about as smart as a Popsicle stick...or have gargantuan balls of steel. Or a death wish, he supposed.

"I bet it was that dastardly Mayor Harlinger," Miss Clara continued. "She's been after this town for years."

Dastardly?

Pieville's Mayor Harlinger was a kindhearted seventysomething woman who originally hailed from the Deep South, which she loved to tell everyone about as often as possible.

"Miss Clara," Ava said, grabbing the woman's hands to get her to focus.

And thank goodness for that, Zach thought, since he had no idea what he was supposed to say after the "dastardly" comment.

"I know this is incredibly upsetting," Ava continued. "I'm upset too—and I can't imagine what Captain Applebottom is going through, but if we just think for a moment, we'll all realize that if someone has actually taken him, it's probably because they love him so much and just want a little quality time with him."

Miss Clara blinked at Ava a few times. "You might be right," she said. "Captain Applebottom is a good, good boy, and he loves everyone. But—" tears starting to glint in her eyes "—but what if I never see him again? He's everything I've got in this world."

If asked, Zach would never have admitted it, but he had to swallow a bit of a lump forming in his throat.

Over a chicken.

But damn it, he was a pretty cool chicken. And Zach had no idea how he would ever tell Chloe if something bad happened to Captain Applebottom. The girl had a soft spot for every animal she'd ever met.

"And you're sure the cage wasn't accidentally left open?" he asked, bracing for the full impact of Miss Clara, who let out a tired sigh.

"Of course I'm sure the cage wasn't accidentally left open."

"And there was no ransom note or any other clue?" Zach continued, quite bravely, if he did say so himself.

"I'm pretty sure I would have noticed something like that," Miss Clara answered, and to her credit, she barely even rolled her eyes.

Zach figured he'd better not press his luck by mentioning the unhelpful thought about vagrant coyotes that happened to be flitting around in his mind.

"Come on," he said, holding his elbow out to Miss Clara. "Why don't I walk you home? It's going to be a long day for everyone tomorrow, especially Ava here, and we should all get some sleep. None of us will be any good for—" he cleared his throat "—Captain Applebottom if we don't get some rest."

Miss Clara nodded absently. "Yes, I need to be at my best for the captain," she said. "He's going to need me more than ever tomorrow."

Zach turned back to give Ava a wave good-night, trying his best not to wish it was a very different woman walking out on his arm.

Ava waved and mouthed a quick *thank you* as Zach escorted Miss Clara out of the store. She had a few things left on her list of things to do before she crashed for the night, but if she hurried, she figured she could still get in six solid hours before the alarm went off again. In about equal measure, she was both thankful and bummed that the Apple Cider Festival only came around once a year.

And even with the drama of the day, she still had the baking contest to think about. Sure, the Apple Butter Glazed Spiced Pecan Blondie could be a contender, but she didn't think it had quite the wow factor to win. And being the owner of the town's bakery/coffee shop, she had to make a good showing, or she'd never live it down. And frankly, it wouldn't be great for business, either. Not that it would stop people from coming—she was the only bakery in town, after all—but it would be a year of listening to people be all like, "This is okaaaay, but it's not like she won the contest or anything," and trying to get Ava to lower the prices on her "subpar" baked goods. On top of that, depending on who did win the contest, there could be an entire year of razzing to put up with, and Ava had to admit there were people in Ambrosia Falls she'd gladly take a razzing from, and people she would prefer…um, not to.

But she was way too tired to think up any more apple-liciousness tonight, even if she only had a few more days to figure it out. Maybe her subconscious could work on it while she slept.

Ava lowered the blinds, locked the front door and turned off the lights as she made her way through the kitchen to the back door, where her car was parked. She grabbed her purse off the coatrack and came to an abrupt halt.

The back door wasn't locked. Which was completely weird, since the back door was always locked. The kitchen was often empty since she spent so much time out front with customers, so she never risked having it unlocked. And as far as she knew, no one she ever had as extra help on busy days had ever forgotten to lock it either. In fact, none of her fill-in staff even used that door. Unless someone had propped the door open to get some air flow or something, but it kind of seemed strange they wouldn't ask first.

Still, nothing else seemed out of the ordinary and nothing seemed to be missing, so Ava made a mental note to talk with the girls about it, then headed home to catch some much-deserved and much-needed z's.

The large floor-to-ceiling windows in the coffee shop made it easy for the Crow to execute his surveillance. These past five years of searching had been the longest of his life, but as he watched from his nesting spot in the bushes across the street, he was finally getting a good look at the Sparrow's every movement.

Sloppy.

Someone like her should know better than to be in the open like that. Of course, it had taken him five years to track her down, so maybe hiding in plain sight wasn't as terrible a strategy as he always assumed.

But none of those thoughts were taking up the most real estate in his mind.

That honor went to the man.

The lackluster nobody of a small-town guy nowhere near exciting enough for the Sparrow. The man who was clearly putting on airs when he made a big show of escorting the old lady home.

Pathetic.

The Crow didn't want him to be of even the slightest consequence—he certainly didn't seem worth it—but after seeing the way the Sparrow interacted with him, the Crow knew something was up. He'd been watching the Sparrow for so long, far before she even knew who he was, far before he'd made her fall in love with him. And if there was anyone on this earth who could read her body language and those sparkling expressions on her face, it was him. He liked to think he knew her better than she knew herself.

Which was how he knew precisely what was going through her mind at that exact moment. She'd be wondering how the darn back door had gotten unlocked. She'd try to explain it away, of course—maybe she'd simply forgotten to lock it herself—but it would niggle at her.

Exactly the way he planned.

He was fine playing the long game. It had been a hell of a long game so far. A few extra hours or days certainly weren't going to bother the Crow. He was a professional who never missed his mark.

Especially now that he'd finally found the only mark that mattered. The mark that had gotten away.

Chapter 4

A couple days later Zach stared out the window, wishing he had a cup of coffee in his hand. It was the same thought he had every morning. He knew he could easily just make it and put himself out of his daily misery, but the payoff when he finally did get that first morning sip was too good to change his routine. Because if he was being honest with himself—something he tried very hard not to do most of the time—he couldn't live without the other payoff of waiting.

Seeing Ava.

Without the excuse of the coffee, he'd have no reason to go to The Other Apple Store until at least lunchtime, and then what would he do with his mornings? Sit at home and try to write? It was plausible, certainly. There was a whole room on the second floor of the house that he'd made into an office. It had an incredible view of the forest behind the backyard, and he'd spent months picking out the right chair that was both comfortable and something he deemed worthy of an author—a high-backed leather number with carved wooden armrests. Any old office chair would not be fit for writing the Great American Novel, after all.

He almost laughed at the thought. He'd never get a word down in that room upstairs. No, he was one of those writers who apparently needed a muse. A damned muse. The notion of it made him feel ridiculous, like a kid who was way too old believing in the tooth fairy, but he didn't know what else to call it. All he knew was after Kimberly left all those years ago, he thought he might never be able to write another word. And he didn't…for a long time. Not until a certain someone moved in next door and all of a sudden Zach felt an itch in his fingertips to write again.

On the days he was being *very* honest with himself— an extremely rare occurrence if he could help it—somewhere deep down he understood it was really that he'd finally found another person who was not so much a muse, but more of a "reason" to do what he did. An inspiration to do something productive with his life. Someone to impress, he supposed. And whenever Zach was around Ava, he simply wanted her to see how hard he was working, which, in turn, made him actually work hard. A convoluted way of getting things done, but effective nonetheless.

Of course, these were all fleeting thoughts Zach routinely pushed way the hell back to the far reaches of his mind, preferring silly notions like muses to explain the phenomenon of his productivity around certain…important people. Not that he'd ever tell another soul about the muse theory either, but it helped him reason away all the time he spent close to Ava.

All those unwelcome thoughts moseyed through his mind as he stared out his front window looking over at Ava's place. Another thought about the fog tried to weasel its way into his brain—something about it being out of place on the warm morning—but it didn't have a chance to settle in before his thoughts turned back to their previous subject. She wouldn't even be there at this hour, but still, he couldn't help but wonder what she was doing at that exact moment.

She'd have gone into the shop to start the day's baking a couple of hours ago already—he always heard her car door slam in the mornings. He knew she tried to be as quiet as possible, and he'd told her the thousand times she'd asked that he never heard a thing, but the truth was, over the years his sleeping pattern had adjusted itself so he would be awake to hear it. Not that it would ever happen in a million years, but it wouldn't hurt to be on similar schedules with Ava for…whatever reason might present itself down the road. Plus, you know, early bird, and worms and everything.

He allowed his mind to wander, an indulgence he only allowed himself once a day during his morning stare out the window, always wishing that bloody cup of coffee he wanted so badly was in his hand.

"Why is it smoky?" Chloe's voice jolted him out of his thoughts…and almost jolted him right out of his skin.

"Jeez, kid, you can't sneak up on an old guy like that."

Chloe rolled her eyes. "Well, if you'd stop daydreaming at the window every morning, maybe you wouldn't be so jumpy. And you're not that old, Dad."

For his own self-preservation, Zach tried to ignore the "that" in her sentence. "I am not daydreaming," he said.

"You were totally daydreaming," she said, and actually patted him on the shoulder. "But it's okay. I get it's part of a writer's job to be all up in your head half the time. Part of the job."

The job. Right. That's definitely what he'd been day-dreaming about.

"So what's with the smoke?" she asked again.

"Smoke?" Zach asked, turning back toward the window.

He supposed the fog did look a bit like smoke.

"Yeah. Since you were staring at it so hard, I thought you would have figured out where it was coming from."

It was a bit strange the way it was hovering there, floating ever so slowly like it was just out for a stroll.

He leaned in closer to the window. "I think that actually is smoke," he said.

"Uh, yeah," Chloe said—for a ten-year-old, she really did have the sarcasm of a teenager already. "That's why I was asking."

Worry started to fill Zach's mind. Where the heck *was* it coming from? Suddenly he realized there were few explanations for the smoke that could end well.

"Come on," he said, handing Chloe her lunch as she was grabbing one of Ava's famous apple cinnamon bagels off the counter for breakfast. "We can check it out on the way to school."

Chloe let out a groan. "I don't see why we have to go to school when the only interesting thing that ever happens in this town is happening."

It was the biggest point of contention between the adults of the town and their kids. All the kids figured the Apple Cider Festival should be held before school started up again, not two weeks afterward. Of course, the real point of contention was really that most of the kids simply wanted an extra couple weeks of summer vacation, but that was never going to happen.

"It's not my fault the apples aren't ready in time," Zach said, using the same old line his parents used to give him when he complained.

They hurried out the door, the smell making it even more obvious the haze was definitely smoke and not fog. In fact, Zach couldn't believe he'd thought it was fog at first, or that it took him until Chloe said something to figure it out, but that was kind of what his brain was like when he was letting it run wild. Far too focused on one thing, the rest of the world falling away. It was why he only let his mind go there once a day, then pushed those thoughts aside for the rest of the time. Mostly.

Zach took the long route toward Main Street since much of the direct route was blocked off for the festival. All of Main Street was blocked off as well, but he wanted to get close enough to see what might have been on fire.

"At least it's not getting worse," Chloe said, saying the exact thing Zach was thinking.

"Yeah, couldn't have been too bad," he said, hoping it was true.

Still, it was a fair amount of smoke—it had to be something more than a barbecue or something.

The smoke began to dissipate a bit as they neared the center of town. The fire had clearly been put out, and there seemed to be just a bit of smoldering going on. Still, Zach couldn't help the knot balling up in his stomach the closer they got. There were too many buildings in the way to see for sure where it was coming from, but the smoke seemed to be located somewhere near The Other Apple Store.

Almost immediately his brain started to go off on a tangent about Ava and what would happen if she were in some kind of danger, which of course sent him spiraling to the moment when the water tower had fallen all over again. He swallowed hard, hyperaware Chloe would be able to pick up on any fear, and she'd already seen enough of his panic over the past couple days.

He cleared his throat, hoping to dislodge the lump sneaking up out of nowhere, and pulled his truck over to the curb as close as he could get to Main Street. Which wasn't all that close since he and Chloe were definitely not the only people who wanted to see what the heck was going on.

"Stay put," he said to Chloe, whipping his door open.

"But I want to see!" she said, putting on the "I can't believe you're doing this to me" voice that usually made Zach want to give her everything she'd ever asked for and then some, which was also the surest indication he absolutely should not do anything of the sort.

But he somehow stuffed his panic down long enough to turn back to Chloe. "I'm sorry, sweetheart, but I need to make sure everything is safe before I let you get near where the fire was, okay?"

Chloe did not look at all pleased, but she knew there was no convincing him otherwise when there was even a sliver of a question over her safety at stake. She sighed heavily. "Fine."

"Thank you. Please lock the doors behind me."

The moment Chloe started to nod, Zach took off down the street, headed toward the lingering bits of smoke, desperate thoughts running through his mind.

What seemed like minutes later, though must have been only a few seconds, Zach rounded the last building blocking his view of the coffee shop. Once he hit the sidewalk of Main Street, he skidded to a halt. The Other Apple Store looked…fine. Exactly as he'd left it last night. But there was something else that was definitely not the same as it had been the night before.

The temporary staging area for the annual baking contest had disappeared. Or rather, burned to the ground. The local volunteer firefighters were on scene and had done a good job of containing the blaze to the staging area, which was no small feat considering it was sandwiched into a small lot between the hardware store and the local insurance place.

Several people were milling around the smoldering area, and it only took a moment for Zach to spot the person who mattered the most.

She would have been just as home in jeans and a tank top, and hell if she didn't look damn good in those, but today she was wearing a sundress, white, with a few lacy bits here and there, and cowboy boots making her look every bit the small-town girl she'd become. Her hair was partially tied back, but it was the pieces that escaped, the ones she was always trying to smooth back, that he liked the most. They always blew in the slightest breeze and he wondered if they tickled her sometimes. Of course, even with those stubborn tendrils, Ava was put together as always, and doing what she did best—helping people. Which that day meant handing out coffees while everyone else stood around in shock.

Zach took a furtive look around to make sure no one

had witnessed his panic, then turned and walked calmly back to his truck.

He had a worried kid to reassure and get to school on time.

Handing out a bit of coffee was the least Ava could do under the circumstances. She was the one who'd had to wake up half the town since she'd been the first on the scene that morning. The timing was strange, although she supposed she didn't know exactly when the fire started, but she luckily noticed it long before it hit its most violent moments. When she'd dialed the emergency line, there had only been a small flicker in the darkness. In fact, it was only because it had still been so dark out that she saw it so quickly.

It almost seemed like the electrical issues were waiting for someone to be there before they made themselves known. Because it had to be something like electrical issues, right? The problem was, no matter how hard she tried to convince herself it was innocent, just an accident, a heavy sense of unease wouldn't let her go.

She'd run out with her kitchen fire extinguisher, but by the time she hung up and gotten the bloody thing off the wall, the fire was in full swing, and she looked ridiculous holding the small canister.

And now she and the team were way behind on the day's baking, not to mention coffee sales were going to be a bit slower considering she was handing it out for free, but it was the least she could do for the town that had saved her life.

Miss Clara stood alone, staring at the charred remains of the temporary staging area.

"Hey, Miss Clara," Ava said, coming up behind her. "Would you like some coffee?"

But Miss Clara looked like coffee was the last thing on her mind. When she turned, Ava could see her eyes were glistening. "This can't be a coincidence," Miss Clara said.

"I'm sure there's an explanation," Ava replied. "It was a temporary stage. The electrical is older and maybe not exactly up to code."

"Maybe," Miss Clara said, "but when you put it together with the water tower and Captain Applebottom…" Her words fell away as she choked up.

Ava had never had a pet, but she could imagine what it must be like to not know where the creature that mattered the most in the world to you was. A pang of guilt shot through her for not taking Miss Clara's loss more seriously last night. Even if the chicken was safe, the poor woman was still going through a terrible time. "I'll help you find him, Miss Clara. Maybe he just needed a break from all the commotion going on."

Miss Clara sighed. "It's alright dear. You've got a business to run. I've got Carol and Eunice coming to help me search down by the river later this morning. If we need more help, I'll be sure to let you know."

"Okay, Miss Clara. But please let me know if I can do anything. Anything at all, okay?" She practically forced a coffee into Miss Clara's hands, feeling like she had to do something, anything, to help pull her out of her misery. Not that the coffee would do much, but it was all Ava had at the ready to give.

Miss Clara wandered off, hunched over a little more than usual and another pang shot though Ava. She made a mental note to have some baked goods delivered to her house later. If anything, maybe Miss Clara could drown her sorrows in a little home-baked comfort.

"We should see what we can do about getting this cleaned up ASAP," Donna Mae from the antique store said, easing up and gratefully taking a cup of coffee. "Or at least covered up somehow."

Ava nodded. "I suppose it won't look good for the tourists if we have a piece of the festival all charred up at the end of Main Street."

"Exactly," Donna Mae agreed.

Just then, something caught Ava's eye.

It was the same damn thing that caught her eye every day. The same damn thing she tried to make sure did *not* catch her eye every day.

Zach.

He was in her favorite pair of jeans, the ones that were just a little snugger than the rest he usually wore. He didn't wear them often—she suspected they were his laundry day jeans—but when he did, Ava made a point of silently appreciating them.

She sighed.

"Mmm-hmm," Donna Mae said, holding her coffee cup close to her lips but not quite taking a sip. A quick glance confirmed her eye had also caught the man in question, still halfway up the street. "I wholeheartedly agree."

"Sorry?" Ava asked.

Donna Mae gave a knowing smirk. "If I were fifteen years younger, I'd be sighing like a schoolgirl when Zach came around too."

Yikes, apparently the sigh had been a lot more audible than Ava thought. She was going to have to work on her reactions when it came to Zach, or she'd have the whole town talking. Although considering they were two of the very few eligible singles in their age demographic in all of Ambrosia Falls, the whole town had probably been talking nonstop about them for years already.

"Donna Mae," Ava said, rolling her eyes." You know Zach and I are just friends."

"Oh, I am aware, but I can't for the life of me figure out why." Her eyes sparkled at Ava as she finally took her first sip of her coffee.

"Hey," Zach said, finally reaching them. "You guys seem deep in conversation."

"Yup, very deep," Donna Mae said helpfully.

Ava cleared her throat and handed Zach the last coffee from her tray. "We were talking about how we should try to mask this whole scene so the tourists don't get antsy."

"Good idea," Zach said. "I don't think we should disturb anything yet, but we could build some kind of temporary fence across the front of the lot to hide it as best as we can."

"You are brilliant," Donna Mae said, eyes still sparkling as she gave him a playful swat on the forearm. "I'll leave it up to you all to figure it out." With that she was off like a rocket. A very satisfied rocket whose job there was done.

People in town were always doing that. As soon as Zach joined a conversation, they would make some weird excuse and hightail it out of there. Of course, it happened just as often when Ava joined some conversation Zach was having. If Ava didn't know any better, she'd think the whole town was trying to get the two of them alone as much as possible. Which was absurd considering all the time the two of them spent in the coffee shop when Zach was there working and Ava was holding down the fort.

"Why, whenever there's something to do in this town, does everyone else disappear and we're left in charge?" Zach asked.

Ava made a murmuring sound. "I'm going to take it as a compliment. We're the ones everyone thinks are the most capable."

Zach's retort was less of a murmur and more of a grumpy growl. "I think everyone around here might be a little too lazy for their own good."

"Well, the vast majority of them are retirement age so I suppose they've earned it."

Zach tilted his head in agreement. "At least the hardware store is right there. I'll run in and see if Jackson has any scrap lumber he's willing to donate to the cause. If you can get a couple guys on board to help, we could have it up in less than an hour, I bet."

"See, that's why people leave it up to us. We *are* the capable ones around here," Ava said, shooting him a wink before she headed back to the coffee shop to refill her tray. Maybe she'd be able to bribe a guy or two with some morning caffeine.

She couldn't help but smile as Zach let out another grumpy groan before he headed off to see Jackson, wondering if it was weird that the sound soothed her.

Twenty minutes later Ava was back in the kitchen making a batch of her famous Choco-Jumble cookies, which were pretty much basic chocolate chip cookies except they were her way of using up all the extra bits and chunks of leftover chocolate at the end of a baking day.

There was nothing apple about them, so she wouldn't be putting them out in the display case for this week, but they were Zach's favorite, and she decided they could be a special treat to reward the guys building the fence.

Once they were in the oven, she headed to the front of the shop to check the progress of the fence. Amazingly, they were almost done with it. Perfect. The cookies would be ready just in time, and they could have them while they were still warm out of the oven.

Her eyes gravitated, as they so often did, over to where Zach was working. Some of the other guys had shed their shirts as the morning sun's rays got stronger, but sadly, Zach was still fully dressed. She'd only seen him with his shirt off once in all the years she'd known him—the time she happened to be at the pool when Chloe had Lil' Duckies swimming lessons and the parents had to be in the pool with the kids. She didn't know Zach well back then, but that didn't stop the moment from leaving a mark on Ava's memory.

She'd been waiting for an encore presentation ever since.

Stop. Just stop, she scolded herself. She could not go there.

Yes, of all the people in the world who could be trusted with someone's heart, Zach was at the top of the list. But she'd thought that about someone else once before, and look where that got her. Though from her view out her window, the way Zach had bent down to hold a board in place while someone else wielded the drill, the place it had gotten her wasn't so bad.

She tilted her head a little. Not so bad, indeed.

Not sure how long she'd been staring, she blinked

when Zach stood up and looked straight at her, giving her a little wave. Caught staring, she had no choice but to sheepishly wave back, dying a little inside, then force herself to get back to work.

Chapter 5

Once the temporary fence was done, Zach eased into his regular booth, laptop in hand. No one else in town even bothered trying to sit there anymore, which made it feel like the spot sort of belonged to him. He liked the thought of a little piece of Ava's place belonging to him.

Ava set down a plate of four cookies.

"Holy mother of all things majestic. Choco-Jumble. You are a goddess," he said.

And even though it was only a silly little remark, Ava gifted him with a smile that could flash-melt the heart of a snowman.

It seemed like everything had been weird lately—the tourists, the town, the strange occurrences, but one bite of a Choco-Jumble and the world was made right again. He tried not to let out a moan of ecstasy, but it didn't work out.

Ava shot him a little smirk, but then her face morphed into something else. Intrigue? Nah, maybe she just had gas or something.

Once all the other cookie bandits/fence builders had left and her helpers in the kitchen were gone for the day, Ava came to sit with Zach.

"Give me a sec," he said, typing in a sudden flurry

until he finished the section he was working on—things never did turn out the same if you didn't finish the thought in the moment—then flipped his laptop closed. "What's up?" he asked.

"Nothing really," she said. "I just…" She trailed off.

"You just what?" he asked, after her pause became less of a pause and more of a longish silence.

"I don't know. It's just—" She sighed. "Is all of this starting to feel a little fishy to you?"

"Fishy?"

"Yeah. Like with the water tower. And Captain Applebottom. And now the contest staging area. All of it put together, it's…starting to feel a little less like a coincidence than I would like."

Zach worked his jaw, staring at her for a minute. He'd been trying all day to push the same thought from his mind, but his brain wasn't having any of it. "The same thought crossed my mind," he said. "I guess I was hoping I was the only one who thought so."

Ava let out a long sigh. "Same here. But at least I feel like I'm not overreacting if someone else thinks so too."

"So what should we do?"

"I don't know. I mean, if anything else happens, I'll feel bad if we don't do anything."

Zach nodded. "You ever get the feeling we hold the fate of this whole damn town in our hands?"

Ava laughed a little, and the sound was like magic being injected straight into his veins. He hadn't meant to use the word "we," like they were in this thing—this moment? this situation? this life?—together, but truthfully, he quite liked the idea of it.

"It is starting to feel like a 'what would they do without us?' scenario," Ava said, still smiling.

"Well, as much as I love this town, how about we do something about that?" he said.

"What are you thinking?"

"I think it might be time to get the authorities involved," Zach said.

After another pause, and some weird expressions weaving their way across Ava's face—he knew every one of those expressions, but he was pathetic at trying to decipher them, even after all these years—she finally conceded. "Yeah, I guess it's time."

Zach pulled out his phone and searched for the authorities in the nearest city. The place was only two hours away, but he suspected a few small incidents in Ambrosia Falls would barely register a blip on their radar. They might even garner a chuckle or two. He'd bet his life what they considered a serious incident was a whole lot different from what the people of his town did.

Still, like Ava said, if something even worse happened and they hadn't at least tried, they'd never be able to forgive themselves.

"Sheriff's Office," came a gruff voice from the other end of the line. The kind of voice that made a person want to immediately hang up for fear they've done something wrong.

But Zach steeled himself and cleared his throat. "Uh, this is Zach Harrison out at Ambrosia Falls."

"Ambrosia what?" the guy on the other end said more impatiently, if that was even possible.

"Ambrosia Falls. Small town about ninety miles north of you. You're our closest law enforcement office."

"Okay?" the man said, making it sound like a question.

"So yeah, anyway, we were hoping you could send someone out to investigate a few incidents that have happened out here over the past couple of days."

There was a hearty sigh on the other end of the line. "And you're sure you're in our jurisdiction?"

"Yes, sir, I'm sure," Zach said, shooting an eye roll Ava's way.

By the look on her face, she was having a grand old time. Honestly, he should have made her call. He'd bet anything that she'd be more successful at convincing these guys to show up. Unfortunately, it was a bit late to decide that now.

"Fine. Let me get something to write on."

He covered the phone with his hand. "He's getting something to write on," he whispered to Ava, whose eyes widened in what seemed to be a surprise/confused combo.

"How could they not have something to write on by the phone at a sheriff's office?" she whisper-yelled with over-the-top drama thick in her voice and a laugh behind those gorgeous deep brown eyes.

"Alright, what is it?" the guy asked.

The guy's voice was something to marvel at, and Zach wondered if he should put the call on speakerphone so Ava could get the full experience of it too, but he decided against it, doubtful whether they'd both be able to keep a straight face.

"Okay, well," Zach began, the guy had a knack for making a person feel nervous, "we have the annual Apple Cider Festival in Ambrosia Falls every year and due to the increase in population, we always have a temporary water tower installed and filled, and the other day the water tower toppled over, nearly taking out a few of our citizens with it."

"How many were injured?" the man asked.

"Well, we got lucky, and no one was injured," Zach said.

"No one was injured," the man said, his waning patience becoming a substantial component to his voice.

"That's correct," Zach said, forging on. "But that isn't the only thing. We also have this makeshift stage where we host our annual Apple Cider Festival baking contest, and this morning it burned to the ground."

"A makeshift stage," the man said.

Zach couldn't help but be annoyed with the way the man kept repeating his words back to him, only in a way that seemed to imply Zach was the biggest chump in the world for bothering him with such petty matters.

"That's right."

The sigh on the other end was even heavier this time. "And did anyone in your—" he cleared his throat "—little town there, bother to take a look at what you think the cause of these…incidents might be?"

"Um, yes."

"And what did y'all come up with?" he asked.

"Well, the water tower seemed to be in a bit of disrepair and so at first we didn't think much of it, but now with the fire, it seems a bit suspicious."

"Uh-huh," the guy said. "So…just so we're all on the same page here, you've had a decrepit water tower, which you only fill once a year, fall down, and then you've had a fire that originated on…what did you call it, oh yes, a makeshift stage. Is that correct?"

Zach was starting to get annoyed with the way this guy was treating the situation. "Right. And there was a third incident as well."

"A third incident, you say. Well, I am utterly on the edge of my seat."

Zach sighed. "Our festival mascot was stolen."

"Your mascot."

"Correct."

"Like, some stuffed apple or something?" the guy said, clearly amusing himself.

"No, our mascot is a live chicken. Um, his name is Captain Applebottom."

This was the point when the laughter started, followed soon after by an alarming amount of wheezing. When it all finally subsided and the guy caught his breath again, he came back on the line.

"Okay, sir, uh," he said as the sound of a page being flipped came over the line, "Zach. I have your number here on the call display. I can't say when we might be able to send someone out to investigate your water tower situation, or your little fire, or," he said, clearing his throat again, "the disappearance of Captain Applebottom—"

Another pause ensued for a bit more laughing, and Zach tried to keep his cool. By the heat in his neck, he had the distinct feeling his annoyance might have been close to reaching the surface.

The man took a few deep breaths to compose himself before continuing. "But I'll be sure to send someone out to your neck of the woods as soon as we can spare the resources."

"Yeah. Thanks," Zach said with little feeling and hung

up with even less hope that anyone would ever actually arrive.

"That did not sound promising," Ava said.

Zach shook his head in both frustration and disbelief. "Sounds like it could be days before anyone even thinks about coming…if they decide to come at all."

"Incredible," Ava said. "What if something actually urgent ever happened?"

Zach shrugged. "I guess we're on our own."

She shook her head a little. "Well, I guess I should get back to it. The display case is looking a bit sparse after the lunch rush. Better go see how much stock is left back there and get a start on some fresh batches for the late afternoon crew."

"Sounds good. I'll just be here," he said, motioning to the general area of his booth. "If that's alright with you."

"Wouldn't have it any other way," Ava said, making something swirl a little in Zach's stomach.

And that was when—right after Ava disappeared behind the kitchen door and Zach had barely opened his laptop again—the worst sound he had ever heard reached his ears.

The sound of Ava's blood-curdling scream.

Flashbacks of the night five years ago flooded Ava's brain. Pain. So much pain. She'd forgotten what that kind of burn felt like. She hoped she'd never feel it again.

Zach burst through the kitchen door, his eyes frantic, searching.

"I'm okay," Ava said, "I'm okay."

But with the amount of pain she was in, she honestly

wasn't sure she was okay. The last time she'd felt this kind of pain, she'd been pretty far from okay.

"Show me," Zach said, his voice gruff and demanding.

But there was only fear in his eyes. A fear that hit somewhere deep inside Ava, making her angry that she was the person who caused fear in this man she cared for so much, but also elation that she had the power to make him feel so deeply.

She held her arm out to Zach, who took it gently, peering closely.

"What happened?" he asked.

"I went to check my phone and leaned on the counter with my arm. Except it wasn't the counter, it was the stove I guess, and the burner was on."

"How was the burner on when no one was even in here?" Zach asked, though he was only half listening, clearly far more concerned with inspecting her arm.

"I don't know," Ava said. "It's never been left on before. And I can't even think what the girls might have been using the stovetop for this morning."

In her mind, Ava began to go through the list of baked goods on the menu that day.

"Here, sit," Zach said, pulling up a stool, then turning to the cupboard where he already knew the first-aid kit was kept, having had to grab a bandage every now again, usually for Chloe.

Ava did as she was told, her mind still taking stock of the morning's menu items. "No, there was nothing that needed the stove. The filling for the Candy Apple Glazed Donut Supreme was made ahead of time. I can't figure out why anyone would have turned it on."

"Could someone have bumped it?" Zach asked, coming back to face her, taking her hand gently again.

Ava shook her head. "I don't think so. You have to sort of push in the knob before you turn it. It's a safety feature meant to stop accidents from happening."

"You're lucky there wasn't another fire," Zach said, checking through the contents of the first-aid kit.

"Yeah, I guess so," Ava said, though something about Zach's words sent a sliver of dread down her spine.

"We should clean this," Zach said, gently guiding her off her stool and over to the sink as Ava's mind kept whirling.

The cool water sent a new wave of pain through Ava, shocking her back to the present. He was so close, using his hands to lather the soap before gently rubbing them on the burn. The gentle pressure momentarily hurt, then subsided as she closed her eyes, concentrating on how his hands felt on her skin. How gentle he was.

This close, she could smell him, a woodsy clean scent she'd come to associate with comfort, though she didn't often get to be so close to it, and she couldn't help but lean in a little more.

"Come," Zach said, and there was so much feeling in the single word as he pulled her gently back toward the stool.

She opened her eyes as they moved, and suddenly the room felt thick with emotion, so thick she could barely breathe.

And so of course she went and ruined it by speaking. "Well, with this and the stage burning down, I guess I won't have to worry about the baking competition." She let out a slight chuckle.

Zach drew his attention away from her hand to her eyes. "Were you seriously worried about it?"

She shrugged. "I always want to make a good showing since I'm the one charging for my baked goods in this town."

Zach grabbed a roll of gauze from the kit and looked directly into her eyes. "Ava, it wouldn't matter what you came up with for the competition. You would have won."

"That's not true," she said, but he cut her off quickly.

"You've won the past five years in a row," he said.

"Only because I stress over it for months in advance," she said. "Except this year, all the stressing didn't even do me any good."

His brow furrowed. "I never knew that about you," he said. "You always seem so carefree. I didn't think you stressed over anything at all."

If only he knew.

"Sorry to burst your bubble," she said, then put her best carefree face back on.

Well, as carefree as someone who'd just burned the hell out of her arm could be, anyway.

But Zach just made a murmuring sound and got back to work, carefully spreading a thin layer of antibacterial ointment across her forearm. His hands were soft and gentle and felt like they always belonged there…touching her skin. She had a brief thought, wondering how she could have survived this long without that touch to soothe her, and she realized then she never wanted to let the feeling go.

He laid a nonstick sterile pad over the worst of the burn and began to wrap it with gauze, careful not to hurt her. The concentration on his face, so careful, the way he bit his lower lip drawing her attention there, his bottom lip full and looking so soft.

She wondered what his lips might taste like.

Heat began to build deep in her center and she closed her eyes again, inhaling deeply, wanting to savor the moment, knowing she'd want to look back on it for a long time to come.

"Does it hurt?" he asked, and Ava realized he was finished with the bandage.

She blinked her eyes open, and he was there, right in front of her, still holding her arm, taking care of her.

"Hey," he said, his voice so soft. He tilted his head slightly, with a little smile, like he was wondering what was going on in her head.

"Hi," she said, giving him a tiny smile back.

They stayed like that for a moment, volleying silent questions back and forth with their eyes until one of them—Ava didn't know if it was her or Zach, maybe it was both—closed the small gap between them, their lips finally, blessedly meeting.

Ava's mind filled with thoughts. Was this really happening? After all the time spent wondering, resisting, pushing him out of her mind, he was finally here, right in front of her. The moment was surreal and unbelievable, and felt like she had finally found a home in this world.

Zach wrapped his arms around her, deepening the kiss as Ava leaned into him. She let go and fell into the abyss of nothingness that could only be found in the safety of someone who was trusted so deeply the rest of the world suddenly didn't matter at all.

He pulled her closer, onto the very edge of the stool, though it felt like she'd never been so stable in her life.

Her arms wrapped around the sturdiness of him, one hand moving down the taut muscles of his back while the other was desperate to find his head, to pull him closer.

And that was the moment the cruel world came crashing back down on her, the pain searing through her arm, shocking her back to reality. A small, gasping wince escaped her lips before she could stop it.

Zach stiffened and pulled back, though he kept his arms around her. Still protecting. Always protecting. "Are you okay?" he asked, the concern heavy in his expression.

"Yeah, sorry. Just forgot about the arm."

And she wanted to keep kissing, to fall back into the oblivion of a first kiss that makes you feel drunk, but the moment was broken. Zach smoothly propped her back onto the stool and pulled away from her.

The moment his touch was gone Ava missed it, and was only slightly consoled when he took her bandaged arm, inspecting it once more.

"It looks okay," he said, finally meeting her eyes again.

"Okay," she said, unsure where everything was supposed to go from there.

Holy shit. She had just kissed Zach. Like really kissed him, and now everything was going to change. And it felt so right, like the change was going to be an incredible thing. But she was scared too. What if he had gotten caught up in the moment and didn't feel the same way about her? What if he regretted it already?

But the thing was, he didn't look like he regretted anything. He looked…happy. Or maybe her happiness was oozing out all over the room and coating him too. Maybe his wasn't even real at all.

Except there had always been…something between them. The kind of thing you knew you couldn't act on until you were ready. Until the time was right. Until all the stars aligned.

And damn if it didn't feel like every star in the universe had lined right up especially for them.

Hadn't she always known they were putting off whatever was going to be between them because they knew as soon as that "whatever" started, it was going to be forever?

She looked down at her arm, which Zach had been holding, then looked at him. He looked like he might have been having the same sort of thoughts running through his mind, but didn't quite know what to do with them either.

What he did do was take a step back, then put his hands into the back pockets of those fantastic jeans and sort of lean back on his heels. "Um, so…" he said, trailing off and looking toward the door to the front of the shop.

Ava tried to smile, but it ended up a little sheepish. "So," she said back, shifting slightly on the stool.

The moment stretched into oblivion.

She opened her mouth to say something, though she had absolutely no idea what that something might be— she just felt like she needed to fill the silence. But Zach apparently had the same thought at the same time, and they both spouted some incomprehensible jumble before each stopped short.

"Sorry, you go," Ava said.

"No, you go," Zach said.

"Um, okay, except I have no idea what I was even going to say." She smiled.

And then he smiled back. "Me neither."

Her shoulders relaxed. He was still Zach. Her best friend.

"So… I guess that happened," she finally said.

He let out a chuckle and pulled his hands from his pockets, taking a tentative step toward her. "Um, yeah. It really did," he said.

Ava thought he was going to come back to her, to give her the one thing in the world she wanted most, which was obviously another long, and hopefully even more passionate kiss—if that was even possible—when his eyes suddenly went wide.

"Is that the right time?" he asked.

Ava's eyes followed his to the clock on the wall. "Shit, Chloe."

"I gotta go," he said, and turned to dash out the door, but just before he reached it, he turned and ran back to her, grabbing her face in both hands and kissing her hard. It was a kiss that said everything Ava needed to know. Because it felt more like a promise than simply a kiss.

She smiled as he dashed through the door.

And smiled as he yelled, "I'll see you later!"

She was still smiling as she heard the tinkle of the bells above the shop door letting her know he had gone.

But then the smile faded as she spotted something on the floor near the other door. The back door. Something had been slipped underneath. But that couldn't be right. It was an outer door, sealed off. And she was sure it hadn't been there when she'd come into the kitchen and burned herself, which meant someone had opened the door while she and Zach had been right there.

Dread oozed up and filled every corner of the room

as Ava moved carefully toward the envelope, picking it up from the floor before she could give herself time to talk herself out of it. A quick glance told her the door was sealed tight and locked.

The dread grew thicker as she slipped her finger under the sealed end of the envelope and ripped, pulling the contents out.

And in that moment, she knew, without a shadow of a doubt, she would never kiss Zach again.

Chapter 6

Zach wasn't sure if it had been the best thing that could have ever happened to him, or the worst. Thoughts about how everything started to go south with Kimberly the moment they started being more than friends filled his mind with every doubt imaginable.

But Ava was not Kimberly.

Maybe this time could be different.

And he had to admit. This time felt different. He was feeling things he'd never felt with Kimberly. Maybe it was because he'd known Kimberly his whole life that the relationship didn't carry the same kind of...spark. That was the only word he could think of to describe it. And my God, did the kiss have some spark in it, although it would be better described as lightning, if he was trying to be as accurate as possible.

He'd thought of a kiss like it so many times, pushed away those fantasies just as often and then the moment—the real moment—had completely snuck up on him. Maybe it was the emotional roller coaster he'd been going through when it came to Ava these past few days—the water tower, and then this morning before he knew she was safe from the fire. The last incident with the burn must have been more than his poor heart could take.

Although he wasn't entirely sure if he'd been the one to initiate the kiss or if she had. He was damned sure thinking about it, that was for certain, but he didn't know who'd actually closed that last, tiny, excruciating gap.

But it wasn't just the kiss that felt different. It was the way he felt inside too. Like the world had a glimmer to it…a lightness. Like he was invincible. No, like he and Ava together were invincible.

Apart, he was just him. But around her, he became someone he liked a whole lot more.

"What's up with you?" Chloe asked, climbing into the truck. "You're never late. I was starting to get worried, you know."

She wasn't necessarily scolding him, but she wasn't *not* scolding him either. Zach decidedly did not like this new side of her. But he *had* been late and couldn't really give her a good excuse.

"I'm sorry, I lost track of time."

Chloe narrowed her eyes. "You never lose track of time."

"I know. I was helping Ava with something, and I forgot to watch the clock."

"So you forgot about me," she said, and Zach couldn't tell if she was legitimately annoyed or if she was just giving him a hard time.

The kid was way too smart, and way too wise for her age.

"I did not forget about you," he said.

Finally, mercifully, she cracked a grin his way. "So…

you were hanging out with Ava, hey?" she said, a tone of amused curiosity in her voice.

Zach couldn't help but feel like he was right back in grade school alongside his daughter. "Chloe," he said, rolling his eyes.

"And you lost track of time," she said, implying something was definitely up.

Zach sighed. "She hurt her arm, and I was helping her."

Chloe's eyes grew wide. "Is she okay?" she asked, a note of concern in her voice now.

"She's going to be fine, don't worry. Has anyone ever mentioned you worry too much for a ten-year-old?"

"Yes. You, pretty much every day," she answered, shooting him a side-eye. "And like you're one to talk," she said.

"But I'm a creaky old adult. It's my job to worry. For the both of us."

Chloe rolled her eyes. "How about we agree it's nobody's job and both stop worrying? Besides, you're only just starting to get a little creaky around the edges."

Zach chuckled a little, amazed, as he so often was, at this kid of his. "Yeah, okay. Deal."

They drove in silence for a couple blocks, then Chloe spoke, spotting the coffee shop up the road. "Can we go get something from Ava's?"

"Not today kid," he said. "I've got stuff to do at home."

He did not, in fact, have stuff to do at home. But he was worried about what seeing Ava again so soon would do to him. That kiss pretty much wrecked him, and he was worried he might lunge for her again the moment he saw her. Which would not be a good look in front of his kid.

And he definitely wasn't going to stare at The Other Apple Store as they passed. Except he found he couldn't stop himself, feeling like a damn teenager desperately hoping to catch a glimpse of his secret crush.

I am in so much trouble, he realized as he craned his neck even further to watch the store for one more second.

It's over, Ava thought. *It's all over. He's found me and I have to go on the run again.*

She shuffled through the pictures one more time. The first, a shot of her hugging Annie moments after the water tower had fallen. Then one of Ava—before the firefighters had even arrived on scene at the contest stage—holding her pathetic little fire extinguisher, knowing it was pointless. Next came shots of the back door of The Other Apple Store, as well as her stove, which Ava took to mean that whoever left these photos was taking credit for the strange, seemingly unexplainable incidents in her own place of business.

And then the final shot, which must have been taken with an instant camera, of her and Zach, locked in the kiss they had shared just moments ago.

The bastard had been right there.

It had to be Justin, and he seemed to be having a grand ole time toying with her. Just like he always used to do. It was the one thing about him that bothered her back then—the way he seemed to get pleasure out of making his targets uneasy.

She wondered how long he'd known where she was. Had he been lying in wait all this time? Waiting for proof she'd moved on with her life? That she actually had a life—one she wouldn't want to leave.

She supposed the kiss with Zach would have proved to Justin that she wouldn't be willing to go easily. He wanted her to be comfortable and let her guard down before he made his move.

He wanted her to suffer.

Tears came to her eyes. She should have known better. She came into this town vowing never to get attached. Sure, she could have friends, ones she would always hold a bit at arm's length, but she would never really let them into her soul. But so much time had passed. Ava didn't know when Zach had wriggled his way straight into the middle of that soul, but she couldn't deny that's exactly where he lived. And somehow, after one person had gotten in, the floodgates opened and now she was pretty much in love with the whole damn town.

She blinked the tears away. This was not the time.

She had work to do.

First things first. Protection.

She went out front to lock the door, putting out a Back in 15 Minutes sign. It wouldn't keep Justin out if he wanted in badly enough, but she couldn't have people wandering in off the street while she did what she had to do. She moved to the closet where they kept the cleaning supplies, conveniently out of sight from any of the front windows, and pulled up a few of the carpet squares she'd laid down to disguise the hatch, quickly pulling it open.

The space wasn't really a basement—more like a glorified crawl space, but it was good enough for what she'd needed it for.

Things she couldn't let others know about.

Ava collected the items she needed, both for protection and for what she knew she'd have to do that evening, then headed back upstairs and took the sign off the door, hoping it would seem to the town that nothing was out of the ordinary.

She had one last important task. A message to send to one of the most important people in her life. The only person who'd remained from her life from before. The one contact in her old life even Justin hadn't known about.

George.

Ava still didn't know how George had managed it. Pulled her from the flaming bunker all those years ago and gotten her to safety and to medical help. She couldn't imagine the strength it must have taken to go down into a smoke-filled hole in the ground to see if there were any signs of life. Then find the will to pull her unconscious body up the steep stairs and back out to the world again. At the age of seventy-five.

He must have been running on pure adrenaline.

Ava opened the browser on her phone, loading up the Buy & Sell page for an obscure medium-sized town somewhere in the heart of Oklahoma. She'd never been to the town, and neither had George as far as she knew, but the online space was where the two of them had communicated for the past five years. They couldn't risk direct contact, of course—George was aging and sometimes needed medical care, so being invisible was no longer an option for him. Thankfully, Justin still didn't know of George's existence, probably still wondered how the hell Ava ever got out of the bunker alive, and so he was relatively safe. Still, Ava couldn't risk Justin even suspecting she'd had help that awful, fiery night, so they kept their communication on the down low.

Ava quickly went into her routine of computer precautions she always took—masking her IP through a VPN and creating a brand-new, encrypted burner email address that would delete itself the moment she hit Send. It wasn't foolproof, but without the tech experts she used to have at her fingertips, it was the best she could do.

She used the email to set up a new account with the site and logged into the Buy & Sell. George knew what to look for. Avocado pits for sale. Ava had noticed a strange trend of people giving away their discarded avocado pits so others could use them to start an avocado plant. Which struck Ava as incredibly strange considering anyone who liked avocados enough to want to grow them would likely have avocado pits of their own to start their plants, but it was, apparently, a thing. Most importantly, a thing easily skimmed past. And in order to make sure she didn't actually get any inquiries about the avocado pits, she put a price tag on them. A small one, about the cost of an actual avocado, which would deter anyone in their right mind from actually being interested in the ad.

But it was what George knew to look for. If Ava ever needed him, she would post about the avocado pits, and vice versa, which would open up a line of communication difficult to trace. Ava spent countless hours skimming that silly Buy & Sell with only the occasional check-in from George. But it was the way it had to be. Anything more direct would be too risky.

She quickly typed up her ad:

Avocado pits, cleaned and dried, healthy? And ready for planting. UnCompromised pits, disease free. Perfect for all you avocado lovers. Call to arrange pickup.

Ava normally wouldn't be so bold as to add the question mark and capitalize the *c* in *uncompromised*, but it was the only way she could figure out how to get her message across to George. If she had a bit more time, she could think of something better, but of all the considerations in a situation like the one she found herself in, time was the most critical. She needed to know if her friend was healthy, and he needed to know she was compromised.

In truth, George had always been much more than a friend to Ava. He was more like a father figure. He'd been her first handler when she'd become an operative and helped her through those first difficult years. And the years had certainly been difficult. Yes, she'd lost her parents years before and had been a ward of the state for a long time, which meant she didn't have a whole lot in the way of family connections, but still. She had a few friends, and when a person agreed to do the kind of work required—lots of unexplainable travel, frequent changes of appearance, and a sudden influx of money— a person had to let things like friendship go.

Thankfully, George had a huge heart and a soft spot for Ava, and Ava knew no matter what went down in her world, there was a single person she could always count on.

George.

And if anything had happened to him, she wasn't sure she could live with it.

For the next few hours until closing time, Ava waited. The more time passed—each minute seeming like an hour—the more worried she became. The only thing keeping her going was the steady stream of customers thanks to the Apple Cider Festival, a welcome distraction.

She must have checked the Buy & Sell page over a hundred times before she finally got a reply.

All good here, do you need me to come?

Ava felt like she could breathe again, and the weight of about three tons of avocados was lifted from her shoulders. She quickly typed into the Buy & Sell instant messaging window.

Hold tight. I'll keep you posted.

Because before she called in one of the most precious people in the world—especially one who wasn't in the best health—she needed to know exactly what she was up against.

Her first thought was to run. Pack a small bag and get the hell out of Ambrosia Falls as fast as she could. It was exactly what she would have done if she was confident Justin had nothing in the town to hold against her, but Ava realized, with a sick feeling swirling in her guts, there was so much in the town he could hold against her. So many people who mattered.

She shouldn't have let it happen. It was Spy 101—never get attached. Never give your enemy something they can manipulate to get to you.

She'd been sure after being shuffled from house to house as a teenager, and then working diligently not to make personal connections all the years she'd been active, she supposed she didn't think she was capable of those feelings anymore, so they kind of snuck up on her.

It was a monumental mistake, and one she'd regret

for the rest of her life if she didn't make this right. And making it right meant one thing…going back to a life she never thought she'd be a part of again.

She needed to bring Sparrow back from the dead.

Chapter 7

Zach felt like a total creeper staring out the front window. He tried to convince himself it wasn't because he was waiting for Ava to pull up to her house—*just checking to see what the weather's up to!*—but even he wasn't buying it. Thank goodness Chloe was busy doing homework in her room or she'd 100 percent start asking him all kinds of questions.

By now, he knew her schedule almost better than she did, not that he was keeping tabs, or anything, and the strange thing was, she was never this late getting home. He wondered if he should start to worry.

He sighed. Ava was a grown-ass adult, and she didn't need some snooping neighbor wondering what she was up to every waking moment. Even one she'd shared an incredibly passionate kiss with earlier in the day. Heat rose up his torso thinking about the kiss, and he tried to tamp it down by gulping a huge glass of ice water. As fast as he could. Unfortunately, a massive case of brain freeze was all he got for the trouble. Those damn swirly emotions were still lurking in his guts.

But honestly, where could Ava be? Sure, it was possible she had plans with someone else in town, but since

Zach was always at the coffee shop, he usually knew about changes in her schedule. He wondered then, if the amount of time he spent around the poor woman might be considered stalking in some circles. And then he wondered if it was a bad thing this was only the first time he'd even thought to consider the notion. Was he being a total pain in Ava's butt all the time? A flurry of panic whirred through his chest until he remembered the kiss. And the way she was completely comfortable around him. And the way she used him as a guinea pig for her recipes.

No, he realized, if she thought he was a big pain in the butt, none of the above would be happening. Still, as if he were back in grade school, he couldn't help but feel like he was doing things all wrong. That's where his mind went when he was all alone and spending way too much time with his thoughts.

When he was around Ava, he felt different. He wasn't nervous. He wasn't worried. He was just him. She had a way of putting him at ease. Maybe that was why he craved being around her so much.

Well, that and the fact he could spend an eternity staring at her and never get tired of the view.

Another hour passed and Zach began to pace. Normally, he would try to pry Chloe away from her phone and get her to do something with him. But he could barely focus long enough to force himself to walk to the back of his house, before rushing back to the front to check the window yet again.

Finally, well after dark, Ava's car pulled into her driveway next door. He breathed out the longest sigh of relief he'd ever expelled in his whole life, then suddenly

wondered if he'd left his wallet in the car and headed out
to check, careful not to glance her way. The last thing
he needed was for Ava to think he'd been waiting for
her to come home.

Only after Ava pulled into her garage and her car
door slammed, did he allow himself to look up. God,
he was being ridiculous, crushing like a thirteen-year-
old, desperately wanting to find out if she liked him. He
supposed it had been so long since he allowed himself
to go there it was expected, but it didn't stop him from
feeling incredibly silly and lame as hell.

"Oh hey," he said, as she came out of the overhead
garage door, as if he'd only just noticed she was there.

Yup, absolute loser.

Ava looked tired, but eventually gifted him with one
of those smiles that reignited the annoying swirly action in his guts, as she hit the button to close the garage.
"Hey," she said back.

For the past several hours, Zach had been playing
this exact scenario over in his mind, with slight altera-
tions each time it played. Sometimes Ava would come
rushing up and fling her arms around him—those were
the best ones—and sometimes she would saunter up, all
cool-like, with a look in her eye that reminded him they
had an exciting little secret. But in none of those fantasy
scenarios did she look like she wanted to flee.

Which was exactly how she was looking now. Eyes
darting, shifting from foot to foot, and generally seeming as though she was stuck in the most uncomfortable
situation she'd ever experienced. It made Zach feel completely awkward and uncomfortable too.

He rubbed the back of his neck. "So, uh, long day, hey?"

"Yeah," she said, nodding a little too vigorously. "Really long day."

Zach had been hoping she'd expand on where she'd been half the damn night, and reminded himself one more time it wasn't any of his business. A concept he hated with the fiery passion of a thousand Red Hot candies and a chaser of Fireball. Should he bring up the kiss? He wanted to bring up the kiss. Except…she wasn't bringing up the kiss, so he probably shouldn't bring up the kiss. If she wanted to talk about the kiss, she would say so.

She shifted her weight one more time.

And then, right after he decided not to say anything, his damned mouth opened itself and started spewing anyway. "So, uh, this afternoon…" he said.

It was barely noticeable, but Zach swore Ava jolted ever so slightly.

She cleared her throat. "Um, yeah…"

"That was, um—"

"Probably a mistake, right?" Ava jumped in, cutting him off and quite soundly crushing his soul into oblivion.

"Right," he said, with an awkward little chuckle. "A mistake…"

"I mean, because we're such good friends and everything," Ava said, her words picking up speed.

Zach nodded in kind of a full-body way, rocking back on his heels. "Yeah, we, uh, wouldn't want to mess anything up."

"Right! Exactly!" Ava agreed, her words full of over-the-top enthusiasm.

And then there was nothing else to say. Just the two of them standing there, staring at nothing, and definitely not looking at each other.

"Um, so... I should be getting in. Kinda tired...you know how it is," she said, along with another weird nodding routine.

"Right, yeah." Zach shook his head a little. "Sorry to keep you," he said, backing away a step and giving her this strange little wave the likes of which he'd never done in his life.

Zach watched as Ava went up her front steps and into her house. She turned back once, giving him a look filled with regret, making him wonder if she regretted this moment, or the one between them that afternoon.

He went back inside, thoughts racing faster than a bird trapped in a house with the homeowner chasing after him.

"Whatcha doin' outside?" his daughter asked in a small voice, startling him out of the mental hamster wheel.

"Oh..." He looked around.

Why had he gone outside?

"Right, I was looking for my wallet."

Chloe glanced over to the console table by the front door. "That wallet?"

Zach followed her gaze, seeing that his wallet was right in the center of it beside his keys...the keys he was currently holding in his hand and must have picked up from *right* beside the stinking wallet before he'd gone out.

Chloe giggled a little. "A bit absent-minded today?"

Zach forced out a small chuckle. "Yeah, I guess so," he said.

He felt like a damn fool.

But unfortunately, it wasn't because of any wallet.

Ava couldn't bring herself to think about Zach. Walking away from him, telling him the kiss was a mistake… it was, inconceivable. Cruel. Both to her and to Zach.

So she just wasn't going to think about it.

How could she? There was something bigger at stake than his heart.

His life.

The fact that the Apple Cider Festival was going on was in Ava's favor. Every Airbnb and rental property in town had been booked up for Apple Cider months in advance, so Justin would never have found a place like that to stay at. And he would have never held out this long before confronting her if he'd known her whereabouts months ago. Of course, Ava wasn't sure he would have even tried any of the legitimate places to stay anyway. It wasn't his MO.

As the Crow, Justin always thought it was much more badass to hole up in abandoned or unused buildings. Ava had always disagreed with him on the matter, thinking it too risky—it was much easier to spot suspicious activity at a place everyone knew was supposed to be empty, and it had once been a huge point of contention between them. And that day, she decided, it was going to be his downfall, like she always suspected it would be. Especially considering she knew Justin was a bit posh, not likely to use some run-down building as the place he went if there were any other options. And Ambrosia Falls definitely had other options. She could think of at least three gorgeous vacation homes that sat empty this time of year—families who didn't love the crowd of the Apple Cider Festival, but also didn't rent their houses out to tourists.

She had a good idea which houses were empty—she was still the Sparrow after all, trained to remember details—but all evening she'd been confirming with some of the locals. Just "making conversation" in order to substantiate what she already knew.

The rest of the daylight was used to prep for the next day's customers. She knew she'd be out late and would never make it back to the shop early for the morning's baking. So with one last pit stop to give Maureen—her main baking assistant—a key and the code to the alarm system, she headed home to prepare for what was to come.

She'd considered Maureen's safety, of course, wondering if she should be worried about her opening by herself in the morning, but she decided if her evening was successful, there wouldn't be anything to worry about anymore.

Her plan had been coming together for hours. Desperate to find some way—any way—to stay in Ambrosia Falls, she had landed on an idea. One chance she might not have to run. If she were to simply take Justin out, make it so he couldn't hurt anyone she loved, she could go on with her life as it was. She could stay in town, keep everyone safe, and most importantly, figure out what everything meant with Zach.

She didn't take the job lightly. She was a different person than she'd been five years ago, but she still had the training. Still had the ability to do what she needed to do for the greater good. It was just that this time, the greater good was keeping herself and all the people she'd grown to love safe instead of someone else.

Running into Zach outside her house had thrown her off though. Seeing the look on his face when he noticed her there—excited, loving, hopeful…all at the same time—she'd panicked. If her plan for Justin didn't work, she needed to keep her distance from everyone in town. Especially the ones who mattered as much as Zach. Plus there was the little matter of making sure Zach didn't catch a glimpse of the weapons she had concealed around her body. Most people would never notice, but if Zach got close enough to touch her, she'd have a whole lot of explaining to do.

So many feelings had flooded her when she saw Zach—fear something might happen to him, a fierce sense of having to protect him and a heavy dose of straight up lust, something she hadn't allowed herself to wholly feel about him before. But that flipping spectacular kiss had awakened something in her. Something that had been dormant for a very long time.

Had it really been five years since she'd had sex? Good Lord, no wonder her nether regions were churning up a storm of hormones, the likes of which she didn't even remember having as a teenager.

But she had to leave all those feelings behind her.

There was a job to do, and she would only be able to allow those feelings back in if she was successful. It was something she was good at—pushing her own emotions away to do what had to be done.

Ava piled supplies into a large duffel bag. The sooner she could get this over with and didn't have anything to worry about anymore, the better. But her burned arm was not making things any easier. It was amazing how a person could take for granted something as simple as packing without thinking. But with her arm in so much pain, it was no simple feat at all, not to mention the bandage around her arm getting caught in her bag. She thanked her lucky stars that at least it hadn't been her shooting hand.

Once she finally got the damn bag shut, she turned out all the lights in her house, including the outside light. She hoped if Zach or Chloe were watching, they'd assume she'd gone to bed. Not that she thought they'd be paying any attention, but she had to admit, if she didn't have so many other things on her mind, she'd probably be staring out the window toward a certain house, wondering what a certain person inside said house was thinking right at that moment.

Giving it a few more minutes to be sure, she finally slipped out the back door of her house and through the main door to her garage, thinking the whole routine would have been a hell of a lot easier if she'd had an attached garage. After collecting a few more things and stowing them in her trunk, she hit the button for the overhead door, cringing at the loudness. But the noise couldn't be helped.

If she got through this, she thought, she'd get something quieter. Then she realized, if she got through the rest of the night, she would no longer have to worry about it.

As she backed down her drive and out onto the street, Ava let out a long, slow breath, trying to calm her vitals, knowing she would need a steady hand—and a steady mind—for what came next.

She would stake out each of the three properties one by one, starting with the biggest. If Justin was still using the same tactics, chances were he'd pick the fanciest place he could get away with.

She headed to the Williams residence first. It belonged to a kindly older doctor and his wife, who loved to have the place on the river to go boating with their grandkids. There was a cluster of trees on the edge of the large semirural property. That was where Ava headed, parking a half mile down the road where her car would blend in with the others on the street, then made it the rest of the way on foot. Not an easy feat considering the heavy duffle she carried. But the one thing it seemed she had done right was stay in decent shape—not prime form, but decent—which made the trek manageable.

Inside the trees, she set up her surveillance, starting with recording equipment she would leave in case Justin was staying there but not present at that moment, then placing her infrared camera to pick up any heat signatures.

She left her sniper rifle in the bag for now, wanting to get a read on the area and the situation. She sat for twenty minutes, barely moving a muscle. Justin was not there.

She left the recording equipment and made the trek back to her car, scanning the area the whole way. She realized, for all the hunting she'd done before, she'd never known she was the one being hunted. She'd been surveilled back when Justin had been watching her all those years, but she'd been oblivious. It was a very different situation when you knew you were being watched. Every sound, every movement in the shadows had her on edge, and it was starting to play with her mind.

Ava moved to the next house on her list, the Batras place on the other side of Main Street. She didn't know much about the Batras family, only that they came to town about three times a year for a week. She knew them to see them although she hadn't had much chance to chat with the family. But she knew where they stayed. Ambrosia Falls was small enough that most anybody knew where most everybody lived, and she made her way close within a few minutes and surveyed the scene.

There wasn't as obvious a hiding place on this property, since the immediate area was more populated than the Williams place. The park across the street would be risky, but it would have to do.

She made her way to the top fort-like area of the slide, somewhat hidden by the heavy boards all the way around. She'd seen many a kid peeking through the boards, only their curious eyes in view, and now she was about to do the same thing. It was just unfortunate she wouldn't be able to place recording equipment here, since kids would no doubt be back as soon as the sun came up. As it was, she was lucky there were no teenagers hanging in the park that night.

After twenty minutes she was certain Justin was not there. She began to wonder if she had it wrong. Maybe he'd changed his ways, after all, or changed them up since he was dealing with someone who'd once known his routine—but she still had one more place to check.

Lawson's.

This property was the most rural of all, but Ava hadn't gone there first because it had been vacated for the least amount of time. The couple lived in town year-round and loved Ambrosia Falls, but they disliked when the tourists "took over the place." Honestly, they could give old Mr. Grumpy Pants Zach a run for his money when it came to complaining about tourists. They "got the hell outta Dodge," as they liked to say—as often as anyone would listen—the day before the tourists started arriving and were back the day after the festival ended.

Ava assumed Justin had been in town planning and scheming long before the first "strange" occurrence, which didn't seem so strange anymore. But maybe he'd been chomping at the bit and was doing things quickly as ideas presented themselves. It would be the best possible situation really, since it would mean he'd be sloppy, and sloppy was almost always what got a bad guy in trouble.

On foot again, Ava moved in closer to the Lawson residence, her hopes falling the closer she got. Justin would have to be reckless to use this place as his center of operations. It was too secluded, too surrounded by trees—he'd be far too exposed. There were a hundred places Ava could hide and he'd never have a clue she'd been there.

Still, she had to check.

Not worrying too much about where in the trees she settled, she quickly pulled out another set of recording devices and placed them on a tree branch where they wouldn't easily be seen by anyone who happened to be hiking, even though she assumed that didn't happen a whole lot, especially with the Lawsons away. She climbed a separate tree and got her infrared out, her stomach jolting when a very bright, and apparently very warm, figure flashed up on the digital screen.

Someone was most definitely home.

There was always a chance the Lawsons had come home early, but there was only one heat signature—exactly what Ava had been trying to find.

Still, she had to be sure. She was always thorough and didn't make many mistakes. This was not going to be the day that changed.

Her next plan was born when she saw the large rock about ten yards away. The moonlight was strong enough to discern the outline of the large boulder. When she was a kid, she would have loved it. There was something about giant rocks that made her feel like they needed to be climbed and sat on. Being seated on a piece of history, something that had been there for thousands of years felt powerful somehow, especially if it was just high enough not everyone would be able to climb it.

Since she wasn't a kid anymore, Ava didn't have as strong an urge to climb it, but she did wish it was a foot shorter so she could comfortably rest her sniper rifle on it for a stable shot. Then again, nature sometimes had a way of solving problems, and a few minutes later her rifle was planted on that rock, her feet balancing on a large fallen tree. It had taken most of her strength to shimmy over to the rock, but the result was worth it.

She'd have a clear line of sight, and if she could see without a doubt that it was Justin inside those walls, she'd have a clear shot too.

Then, as she gazed through the scope, her heart clenched.

The profile she hadn't seen in years, back to haunt her, as if in a waking dream. And then he turned, facing her fully. She was shocked at how brazen he was, how open and careless he was being. He had essentially announced he was in town. It wasn't like him. Even if he had never been as careful as she was, he'd never been this easy to get to.

Something wasn't right.

But she would never get another chance like this. She couldn't walk away without taking it.

Ava gave herself a few minutes to work through it in her mind, coming at it from every angle, but could not think of a single reason he would purposely be so careless. Maybe he was losing his touch. Sometimes she wondered if he ever had the operative's touch, often wondering if he'd been paired with her back in the day because she would ensure he'd be careful. He was always the brazen one, the one who wanted to charge in without thinking everything through. She'd thought he'd learned a thing or two from her, but maybe he'd gone back to his old ways. His sloppy ways.

Whatever the case, the situation was as it presented itself, and she would not waste this chance at saving the life she'd created these past five years.

She rechecked the wind and stilled her body using the breathing techniques she'd once used on the regular, slowing her heart rate. Justin moved around the kitchen, going from the stove to the fridge to the counter, clearly making a late-night snack.

Still hardly able to believe he was exposing himself the way he was, Ava went into Sparrow mode, clearing her mind of all thoughts, her only focus on the chest of the man inside the house. And then in her mind, the man wasn't a man anymore. And he certainly wasn't the man she'd once shared her life with. Shared every secret with. Almost.

He was only a target. It was the way she was able to get on with what she had to do. Depersonalize the situation. Make it a job. Compartmentalize.

One more slow breath in, and then out through her mouth so slowly, so still…only her finger moving ever so slightly.

The shot was quiet—the silencer doing its job. The only sound was glass shattering as the bullet hit the window and in the same moment, the target went down.

She got him straight to the chest, exactly as she'd intended.

Ava didn't smile. Tried not to think.

It was always that way after a hit. Emotions were tricky things in the moment, and she used all her energy to keep them pushed as far away as possible, focusing on the rest of the job. Putting away her equipment, making any sign of her having been there disappear.

Thankfully, the emotional distress only lasted a short while. Some kind of primal reaction that faded quickly if she didn't let it take hold. By the time she made it into the Lawson house, any residual pangs had wafted away. It was one of the reasons she was good at what she did. Had stayed human enough to stay on the right side—some operatives were apt to switch sides on a whim…or financial incentive—but detached enough to be able to sleep at night. She understood what needed to be done, and not everyone had the capabilities to do it.

Truthfully, she hadn't been sure she was still capable after living in the world she'd been living in the past five years, allowing herself to get close to people again, to let real emotions in again. But it was the same as it had ever been.

She eased into the Lawson house, quickly and quietly. In theory, there should be no one to be quiet for, but it had always been her way. Soft and quiet as a tiny bird, disturbing as little as possible.

She wouldn't be able to clean up completely—the broken glass of the window would stay, but she couldn't leave a body for the poor Lawsons to find. Though as she crept though the house, something felt wrong. She knew it immediately.

And as she moved into the kitchen where all she found was a disturbing lack of a dead body, her heart sunk. She grabbed for the firearm at her side, even as she knew there was no point.

She could feel it as surely as she felt her heart speed in her chest.

The Crow was long gone.

Chapter 8

Zach was at a loss.

He'd practically worn the finish off the patch of floor he'd been pacing for the past two hours, not knowing what to do, trying to convince himself there had to be a reasonable explanation for what he had seen.

Ava sneaking from her house—just an hour or so after she'd told him to his face that she was tired, implying she was headed to bed. And she should have been headed to bed considering she'd have to rise again at the crack of dawn, if not sooner, in order to start her baking for the festival guests.

But that was very much not what she had done.

Zach hadn't meant to be watching, but something in him was drawn to his windows that night, even after he'd turned his lights off and "gone to bed" too. He hadn't really gone to bed. All he'd done was tuck Chloe in, and then head to his room. Yes, he'd had intentions of turning in, but with all that had happened, there was no way in hell he was going to fall asleep anytime soon.

Still, he didn't want Chloe to worry, so he turned off his light and lay on his bed hoping by some miracle he'd actually drift off. But after lying there for a good fifteen minutes with thoughts rolling through his head, picking up speed as if they were on a runaway, downhill trajectory, he was even further from sleep than he had been when he lay down.

And then he heard the noise.

It wasn't a particularly loud noise, but it was very familiar.

For a moment he wondered if he was losing it. Had he fallen asleep and not realized it? Because what he heard was a sound he heard almost every day…but never until morning. Ava's garage door.

He checked the time on his phone.

Not quite midnight. Okay, so he wasn't losing it.

He got out of bed and moved the curtain a hair, just in time to see Ava's car backing out of her garage, down the driveway and out onto the street…all without turning on the headlights of the car.

Which was incredibly weird.

Because she wouldn't have anything to hide, right? And then, in a moment of extreme clarity, Zach realized she did have something to hide. She'd been acting weird ever since the kiss. And yeah, that kiss had changed everything, and maybe Ava was scared of what it meant— God, knew Zach was scared too—but Ava had never been one to hide from what worried her. She was more of a "get it all out in the open" kind of person—something that had given Zach more than his fair share of uncomfortable conversations.

Like the one he'd had the other night with her about Kimberly. The conversation he'd avoided like the plague for years. The one he knew would make him and Ava grow even closer because it was one of those "vulnerability moments," which he hated with the absolute breadth of his being, but apparently one that his subconscious was willing to have because maybe, just maybe, he was ready to move on. And damn it, if he was going to move on, he wanted to move on with Ava.

After Zach paced in his room for twenty minutes, a thousand scenarios running through his head with possible explanations for Ava sneaking out of her house in the middle of the night, he moved downstairs. Much more room to pace there.

But after another hour with no sign of Ava returning, he still hadn't come any closer to an explanation that made any sense.

Why would she feel like she had to sneak out? It wasn't like she answered to anyone, let alone Zach, who was likely the only person who might even notice her leave. He'd never ask that of her. But what was with the timing? All these years, he hadn't let himself go there, then lately, things had started to feel different. Like maybe he didn't have to be alone for the rest of his life. Like maybe, if he gave love another shot, it wouldn't have to end badly.

And then the kiss happened, and everything changed. Like the universe was confirming yes, finally, he could have something good without worrying it was all going to leave him. The kiss felt like a forever. Like everything in the world was clicking into place. Like he'd finally found a way to feel "right" when he'd always felt a little bit wrong somehow.

Zach could feel himself starting to spiral. The thoughts entering his mind barely even made sense anymore, but he was having about as much luck stopping them as he would stopping an avalanche with his bare hands.

He was also starting to feel a sense of panic, an urge to get out into the open air. The house was closing in on him. But there was Chloe to consider. She was usually a heavy sleeper and rarely woke up during the night, but if she did, he couldn't let her find the house empty.

He had an old baby monitor in her room, which he'd been meaning to get rid of for years, but just for one night, he could sneak in and turn it on. But then he'd risk waking her.

He could leave a note, he supposed. He paced some more, trying to think of what might happen if Chloe woke up. She'd probably be headed for the bathroom and then straight back to bed, which wouldn't be an issue. But if she woke up and came looking for him, he'd feel like the world's worst dad if she couldn't find him and thought she'd been left alone. If that was the case, she'd go straight to his room, so he quickly wrote a note saying he'd be out in the front yard.

At least out there, he'd have room to pace. Room for his thoughts to—well, to what, he wasn't sure, but he supposed he hoped they'd leave or work themselves out or something.

He wrote two more quick notes—one for the kitchen in case Chloe went for water, and one he taped to the inside of the front door, in case she somehow missed the other two notes and made it all the way to the point she would head out the door. It was definitely overkill, but he wasn't going to take any chances stressing his kid out.

Outside, the air was cool, and it suddenly felt like he could breathe again.

But the thoughts still swirled, spreading like wildfire, becoming increasingly more intense by the second.

One minute he was almost convinced Ava had just left to check on the stove or something at the coffee shop. The next he was in a full-blown panic imagining Ava being so disgusted by his kiss that she packed up and fled in the night, never to be seen again.

Unfortunately, he couldn't make any of the believable—or even a single one of the truly ridiculous—scenarios add up. It didn't make sense that she snuck out with no headlights if it was something innocuous, like checking the coffee shop, and, well, the wild scenarios didn't fit Ava. She wasn't a runner.

A brief thought flitted through his head. The way she arrived in town had been sudden and unexpected, and for the first time he wondered what the circumstances had been. It hadn't been so out of the ordinary that he thought anything of it at the time, but…could there have been something off about her late in the day arrival? Or the fact he never saw anyone take a look at the house next door before the moment she moved in. Was that a thing? Did people buy houses off the internet without going to see them in person? Seemed like a rash, irresponsible thing to do—and Ava certainly wasn't that. But still, he supposed it was possible.

He rolled a dozen more scenarios over in his head. Reasons someone might buy a house sight unseen. Running from a domestic situation, financial instability—but then, how would one afford a house?—evading the police…

They were all terrible. Unless there had been some sort of bidding war over the house. But he was sure he would have heard about it if there had been. Not to mention the local Realtor, Sandy St. James, was not particularly known for keeping secrets under wraps. Half the town would have kept him in the loop on that one. Hell, probably 99.8 percent of the town, considering it affected him directly, being next door and everything.

He was so lost in his thoughts, still pacing between his house and hers that it took him much longer than it should have to hear the crunch of the gravel on the street, nearing Ava's driveway. There was no way to run back across to his place without being seen, but he didn't particularly love the idea of being caught out there pacing in the middle of the night either.

Ava had made it clear she wasn't interested in being anything more than friends, and pacing in front of her house was a look that was a hell of a lot more stalkerish than Zach preferred.

In a panic, he strode up the steps of Ava's front porch, clinging to the shadows.

And the moment he got up there, he realized he was trapped.

She was still driving with no headlights, and worse, she was already out of the car to lift her garage door manually, he assumed, so it would make less noise.

There was no question. She was absolutely hiding something. Most likely from him.

And, even though his curiosity had never been so piqued, he wished, more than anything, he could disappear into thin air, just for a couple of minutes.

Ava drove into her garage, and Zach wondered if he should make a break for it. Unfortunately, by the time the thought could fully form, she was already coming back out of her garage to close the door again.

He skulked farther into the shadows, wishing he was

back to feeling as creepy as he had staring out the window earlier. Because his "I am such a creeper" factor had gone way up since then. It was shocking how easily he'd turned into an irrational being when all his life he'd been rational as hell.

Ava made her way across the short expanse of grass, then up the stairs, headed for her front door. Zach began to believe maybe, just maybe she would simply go inside and never know he'd been there at all, pleading to the heavens that if he were to escape this humiliation, he would never, ever do anything so stupid again in his life.

Her keys jingled as she reached toward the door, and Zach's heart began to soar. It was happening! He was going to make it out of there unscathed!

And then, in a final second of absolute horror, mixed with a hearty dose of confusion, a light burst on out of nowhere, throwing them both into a dizzying flash of movement and terror. Zach terrified of getting caught, but realizing poor Ava was probably in fear of her life.

Although, as he stared down the barrel of the gun she'd pulled out from somewhere in her jeans' waistband, so fast he'd barely even seen her move, perhaps she hadn't been quite as caught off guard as he thought.

In the split second that passed, Ava fully expected to see Justin's steely blue eyes staring back at her, but those eyes were not the frigid blue she anticipated at all. They were warm and kind and…well, truth be told, looking fairly terrified.

"Jesus, Zach!" Ava yelled, quickly lowering the gun and shaking it a bit, like it was hot and she could only touch it gingerly. "What the hell are you doing? I could have killed you!"

She was out of breath, her heart beating fast after being jolted into action. It was only thanks to her training that she'd taken the nanosecond before she blindly reacted and pulled the trigger.

So close. Way too close.

The thought of losing Zach was too much, but imagining it could have been her own fault made her instantly sick. She moved closer to the porch railing to lean on it, feeling rather unsteady on her feet.

Zach stood speechless for a bit, hands in the air like someone in a damn movie "stickup" scene or something. Slowly, he lowered his hands.

"Um, sorry." He cleared his throat. "Didn't mean to startle you," he said weakly, lowering himself into a nearby chair, looking a little shaky and a little green around the edges.

Ava leaned hard into the railing she'd been clutching, her adrenaline waning fast, suddenly feeling exhausted and wondering what time it was. It had to be at least two in the morning if not later.

"Zach, what are you doing on my porch in the middle of the night? In the dark," she added, to make sure she pointed out how weird it really was. Maybe to make herself feel better for pulling a gun on her best friend.

Who, she realized, after what had gone on earlier, and then over the past couple of minutes, was maybe not actually her best friend anymore.

Zach had been staring at his quaking hands and finally looked up, a little dazed. "Um... I," he said, and looked around like he was trying to come up with some kind of plausible explanation, but then his shoulders dropped, and he let out a long sigh. "This is going to sound dumb, but I was out here getting some fresh air."

"Some fresh air," Ava said, the doubt heavy in her voice. "On my porch."

"No. Well yeah, but…" Zach trailed off again.

"Zach," Ava said, moving to sit across from him. She needed to be at eye level. "Talk to me. What's going on?"

He looked into her eyes then, and Ava wanted nothing more than to close the two-foot gap and latch on to those soft lips again, but there was no way they could go there. Not ever again.

"I just—" he let out another short breath, like he was giving up on trying to make it look like anything other than it was "—I was out here pacing, okay?" he said. "I saw you."

Ava's brows furrowed together, her brain scrambling to figure out what, exactly, he had seen. Her stomach instantly seized, thinking the worst. What if he had seen her shoot at the Lawson house?

"I saw you leave. In the dark. With no headlights on."

Oh.

To his credit, the words weren't accusing, just had a sense of…hurt or something behind them.

"Zach, I—"

He held up a hand. "It's none of my business. And I have no business being here right now either. I don't know what I was thinking." He moved to stand.

"Zach," Ava said, her heart hurting, stretching as if it were trying to reach for him. She should let him walk away—it would be better…safer for everyone—but she couldn't do it. Couldn't leave him like that. Couldn't let him think whatever the hell he might be thinking about her. And the kicker was, it shouldn't matter what he thought. But right then, it was the only thing that *did* matter. "Can you please sit? I... I don't know if we can figure all this out, but can we at least try?"

Zach settled back into the seat and nodded.

Ava looked around, suddenly realizing they were exposed out there. "Where's Chloe?" she asked, trying to keep her voice steady.

"Sleeping," Zach said.

"Let's go over to your place and talk," Ava suggested. "I wouldn't want her to wake up not knowing where you are."

"Yeah, okay," Zach said, and there was still something unsure in his voice, almost zoned out.

Ava let Zach lead the way down the porch steps as she took a long look around, searching for any sign of movement—a flash of metal or glass in the moonlight, an out of place rustling of bushes—but she didn't sense anything.

She probably wouldn't even if there was danger. Justin was usually too good for that.

Which only sent her thoughts whirring again. Had he meant for her to see him back at the Lawson house? He had to have been wearing a vest to have gotten away. There hadn't even been any blood at the scene. Which meant what? Had he planned the whole thing and she'd completely fallen for it?

She felt like a damn fool. And the two of them absolutely, 100 percent, needed to get inside the house immediately and get the curtains shut.

Once inside, Zach seemed to get a little clearer, pulling some whisky out of the cupboard and pouring it into two small glasses while Ava shut the curtains.

"We should move to the living room," she said.

They'd be farther away from windows than at the kitchen table.

Zach didn't argue, just set the glasses down on the coffee table and put his head in his hands, pulling his fingers through his hair slowly before taking a sip from his glass and leaning back heavily into the couch.

After checking each window in the room, making sure everything was shut, locked and covered, Ava finally came to sit across from him.

"Ava, what's going on?" Zach asked. "Why do you have a gun?"

She knew it would be the question on his mind since the moment it had been pointed in his direction, and she couldn't blame him. Guns weren't especially common in the town of Ambrosia Falls, unless someone was using a toy one for a target practice game at the fair.

There was no way out of it, she decided. She was going to have to come clean.

Mostly.

She took a slow sip of the whisky, feeling every inch of the burn from her lips to her stomach, letting it take over and fill her with something, anything other than the dread of what she was about to say.

"When I came to Ambrosia Falls," she said, "it was because I was running from something. Well, someone, I guess."

Zach nodded, like he'd suspected her to say exactly that. He also looked like he was itching to jump in and ask a million questions, but he stayed quiet. Still.

So still it made Ava nervous, and she marveled at how often this man made her nervous. No one had ever done that to her before. No one had ever been so important.

"I was involved with a man," she began, hating how the damn story was already making her sound like a victim. She had never allowed that term to be something used to define her. But she sure as hell couldn't tell him the whole truth. She couldn't bear what he might think of her then. "He was great at first…you know how the story goes. And then he tried to hurt me, and he had powerful allies and so I was put into witness protection."

Zach's mouth opened slightly in surprise, but he remained quiet.

"And, as I'm sure you've guessed, after all these years, he's found me."

Finally, Zach spoke. "So, the fire. And the water tower? That was all…this guy?"

Ava nodded.

"Shit," he said. "He broke into your place."

Ava nodded. "Looks like it."

"And the police are on their way," he said. "Maybe."

"I wish we had never called them now," Ava said. "Knowing what we're up against, the police might be more in the way than they are of help. They'll think this is just some regular guy, not someone trained."

"Trained?"

Ava nodded. "Justin's…well, he's sort of an operative."

There was a pause that went on long enough to make Ava a touch queasy.

"Like CIA or something?"

"Kind of. He's more of an off-the-books kind of operative."

Zach let out a slow breath. "The kind that does the work the sanctioned operatives can't really get away with without certain people and agencies asking too many questions?"

"Exactly."

"So we have one of the world's most dangerous men after us? Here, in Ambrosia Falls?" His voice rose a bit at the end, and as much as Ava hated that she was freaking Zach out, it had to be one of the most adorable things she'd heard in a long time.

"He's not after us," Ava corrected. "He's after me. And I plan to fix that as soon as the sun comes up."

Zach looked a little panicked. "What does that mean?"

"Zach," she said, "I have to leave. It's the only way."

He shook his head, the panic morphing into a resolve that had Ava's heart melting faster than butter on a cooktop.

"No. You are not leaving. We've finally, I don't know, started to figure out what this is," he said, gesturing between the two of them, "and I'm not about to let that go."

A sting formed behind Ava's eyes. The last thing she wanted was to never be able to see it through with Zach, but there was no other way."

"I've already tried to fix it, Zach."

"What do you mean you've already tried?"

"I tried to find him. To take him out." She hated that the way he thought of her was probably changing by the second.

"Like kill him?" he asked, saying the last words in a whisper.

She sighed. "Yeah."

He ran his fingers through his hair. "Why the hell

would you do something so dangerous by yourself?" he asked, his eyes wild.

Ava contemplated coming clean. All the way clean. Contemplated filling him in on the fact that she was more lethal than Justin. That she'd had so many more years' experience behind her. Though that might not be true anymore, considering her experience had come to a standstill once she moved to Ambrosia Falls. She wondered what Justin had been up to since that fateful day five years ago.

"It's fine," she said. "I've learned to take care of myself."

"Well, you don't have to anymore."

"Of course I do, Zach. This is ridiculous. I'll go and everyone here will be safe. I wouldn't be able to live with myself if anything bad happened to the people here. Knowing it was my fault and I could have stopped it by leaving."

"You can't start over all over again," Zach said.

"I can," Ava replied. "I've done it before, and I can do it again."

"Well," he said, breathing hard. "Then I don't think I can start over all over again."

"Zach," Ava said, moving to turn away. She couldn't take the look in his eye. The one saying she meant everything to him. Of course, she only knew the look so well because the feeling was disastrously mutual.

Zach grabbed her arm and turned her gently to face him.

"Like it or not, it's not just you that you have to think about anymore. This town, all of us…we're your family now. And even if nothing more ever comes out of you and me, I'm your family now. You're my best friend, Ava. We're going to figure this out together."

Chapter 9

Strangely, Zach was relieved. He'd obviously known something was up, and the fact it had nothing to do with the kiss made everything okay again.

Well, maybe not everything, considering Ava's life was being threatened by a professional damn spy or whatever, but he'd be lying if he said he wasn't relieved all of it meant that he and Ava might still have a chance to be together.

"Maybe he's already on the run," Zach said. "If you tried to take him out."

Ava shook her head. "I think he knew I was coming. He must have had it all planned out. He's messing with me."

"Jesus," Zach said. "This guy is sick."

"And," she said, "he's not playing by his usual playbook."

"So, what now?" Zach asked.

"The smartest thing is for me to get out of here—"

"Stop," Zach said. "You aren't going anywhere. We just need to find a way to get the cops out here faster."

Ava shook her head. "That will put them in danger too. They won't understand how Justin is. He's smart. He's more dangerous than anyone they've come across before."

She gave him a serious look, like they should give up too, but Zach hadn't waited five years with a massive crush to let it go the exact day he finally decided to do something about it.

"Okay, so where would Justin go?"

Zach hated the way this guy's name sounded in his mouth—he'd honestly love to get his hands on this guy who'd hurt the most important person in his world—but he pushed the feeling aside. For now.

Ava sighed. "In the old days, he would find someplace nice. Someplace that wouldn't be roughing it too much. Let's just say Justin likes his amenities. I found him in the Lawson house."

Zach raised his eyebrows. "He was in Gus and Millie's place?"

Ava nodded.

"So are we looking for another place like that?"

"I doubt it. He knew I was coming. Had taken precautions."

"So he knew you'd know his regular routine and was counting on you coming after him."

"I guess so," Ava said. "I thought he'd be just cocky enough to stick with his routine."

"I'm surprised he'd even think you'd come after him like that."

"Um, yeah," Ava said, shifting a little, like she was uncomfortable.

Zach figured he'd be a little uncomfortable too if something like this suddenly sprung up from his past. And even though Ava was a victim, she thought she was safe and had finally let people back into her circle again. Had finally begun to trust again, and now her whole world was imploding.

And if he knew Ava at all—which he liked to think he did—she would even be a little embarrassed she hadn't been able to take care of it on her own. The woman was nothing if not fiercely independent. It was a quality he admired about her, a quality that, frankly, made him even more attracted to her, but at some point, she had to realize she didn't have to do everything on her own.

At least he hoped she would, since there was nothing he wanted more in the world than to take care of her in every way she'd let him.

He wasn't sure what the hell he was going to do once they found this guy, but he was anxious to make a plan and get it over with. More importantly, he was anxious to get on with his life with Ava. Assuming this whole thing with Justin was the reason she'd blown him off earlier.

Except...what if it wasn't?

Shit.

"Um, can we pause for a second and get something straight?" Zach asked.

"Um, sure?" Ava said, phrasing it like a question.

Zach stood and started to pace. Lord knew he'd done enough pacing for one night, but there was no way he could sit still and say what he was about to say. "Okay. So, the, um..." He cleared his throat and stopped pacing, turning to Ava. "The kiss."

Ava nodded once. "The kiss."

Zach's pacing resumed. "Yeah, so I'm just going to lay it all out there and say I don't actually think it was a mistake. And maybe you still do or whatever, or maybe you said it because of this Justin thing, but I thought we should, like, get on the same page about it."

He stilled. Turned. Looked at her, his heart filled with equal parts dread and hope.

Ava stared back. For what seemed like an impossible amount of time, though it might have only been a heartbeat. And then she smiled. A shy smile Zach had never seen on her—she was always the least shy person in the room—but somehow it made her look more like…herself.

Zach held his breath.

"I don't think it was a mistake either," she said.

Zach felt every speck of stress release from his body in a giant wave of relief, and for a moment, everything was right with the world. And then, knowing the seriousness of the situation they were in—a place where she could be taken from him at any moment—every muscle tightened up again almost as quickly as they had relaxed.

"Okay, good," he said, his voice serious. "Then we have to concentrate on getting this guy so we can, you know, do that some more."

Ava looked like she was working hard to hide a smile, and somehow almost even managed it. "Okay," she said. "Sounds reasonable."

"As reasonable as talking about taking out a guy can sound, I suppose," Zach said.

"Indeed," Ava agreed.

"Okay, so now that we have that out of the way," Zach continued, "I'm guessing this Justin asshole needs another place to hide out then."

"Probably," Ava said, deep in thought.

"Probably?" Zach asked.

"Yeah, but it doesn't matter where he is," Ava said, as she noticed the first traces of the rising sun break past the edges of the curtains in Zach's living room. "Because we're going to make him come to us."

Ava needed sleep badly, but a quick glance at her watch told her it was time to get up. Except she hadn't actually gone to bed. It was a damn good thing she worked in a coffee shop, because she was going to have to be mainlining the stuff for the rest of the day.

"What do you mean, he's going to come to us?" Zach asked.

"It's the one thing he won't expect," Ava said. "He's going to assume I'm either going to run or try to go after him again. And since he's been a step ahead of me this whole time, he'll probably continue being a step ahead of me. So we have to do the one thing he doesn't think we'll do."

"Which is…nothing?"

"Exactly. At least for now until I can work out a real plan. If there's anything I know, it's that plans made under duress or exhaustion are never as good as plans that have had plenty of time to be thought through."

"So, what…we just go about our day as usual?" Zach asked, looking slightly horrified.

"It's me he wants, and I know how to be careful," Ava said.

"There is no way I'm going to let you out of my sight for a second," Zach countered.

Ava only rolled her eyes a little. "You're going to have to let me out of your sight for at least a second. Like, for example, when I go home in a few minutes to shower and change."

His lips twitched up into a half grin. "I mean, are you sure you don't need any supervision for those, um, difficult tasks?"

The thought of Zach watching her shower sent a thrill through Ava's body, but she managed to keep the crimson of her face tempered. "I'm pretty sure I can manage," she said, though she gave him a little smirk back that hopefully said once all this was over, she might be game for some sudsy supervision.

"Okay, I'll let you go get ready for the day, and I'll do the same over here, but you have to stay on the phone with me the entire time."

"Don't you think that's a little overkill?" Ava asked.

"Do I think it's overkill to take the absolute minimum amount of precaution when we know there is a trained killer after you? One which you've recently poked like a damn bear, except instead of just poking him you actually shot him?" He raised his eyebrows as if waiting in great anticipation for her answer.

"Um, okay. You have a point," she reluctantly agreed. "Even though I still don't think he'll do anything."

"But that's what I don't get. Why don't you think he won't do anything?"

Ava shifted. "Because he's toying with me. The water tower, the fire, the pictures he left on my doorstep…" She decided not to let Zach in on the fact that the pictures had actually been left right there in the room while they were busy making out. "I'd bet my life he's not done yet. He has a plan, and if there's one thing I know about Justin, it's that he will not be satisfied unless his plan is acted out to perfection. It's why we're taking today to regroup and do nothing. It's going to drive him to a tizzy wondering what the hell we're up to."

"I gotta say, it's probably not going to be a tizzy-free kind of day for me either," Zach admitted.

"I know. It's going to be tense. But we'll be on alert and make the best of it for now. If we get any time to ourselves at the coffee shop, we'll think about what our next steps will be—maybe even get a chance to talk them through."

Zach nodded. "I don't like it, but I'll agree to your plan."

"Good," Ava said, turning to head to the door.

"I just have one more question."

She turned back and he grinned.

"Would it be okay if I kiss you?"

Ava couldn't stop the smile from creeping across her face. "Um, sure," she said, cool as ever even though her mind was screaming *yes, yes, yes!*

He stepped toward her, then slowed, grabbing hold of her arms lightly, his hands shaking a little.

"I'm so nervous," he said, then let out a little chuckle.

She laughed a little too, her insides vibrating—the excited feeling that made a person shiver as if they're cold. "I'm still me," she said, though the idea made her feel guilty. She was still hiding so much from him.

"I know, that's why I'm so nervous," he said, his face inching closer until finally his lips met hers and she let out a tiny sighing moan, relief flooding over her.

Strange that relief was the sensation she felt, though she supposed she'd been building the moment up for so many years, and then there was the whole roller coaster of the day—yesterday now, she supposed—making every emotion hover so close to the surface that none of them would really be a surprise. Grieving the idea of losing Zach only moments after it felt like she really found him, and then the hope blooming again…it was all so much. And she knew she couldn't quite trust any of it.

Justin had to be dealt with first.

But Ava was determined to savor the kiss, trying like hell to burn it into her mind and make it last forever. But it's funny what the brain did when those moments were happening though. Almost the precise second a person decided they wanted to really remember something because it's so damn good, or delicious, or perfect, that betraying brain tended to check out like a traitor, making the moment fog up and become hazy, leaving only a vague whispery essence of the real thing. It was why Ava knew she would crave that kiss forever.

The kiss was soft, not as urgent as the one in the coffee shop, but still, it felt familiar. Not because it was their second kiss, but because it felt like Zach. This had been exactly the way she'd imagined being with him would be. Sure. Steady. Gentle, but strong at the same time. Where the first kiss had been a whirlwind, a frenzy, this one felt a whole lot like being safe.

Of course, brains didn't only betray with memory, but with recollection too. And again, with its precise timing, the moment even the idea of safe popped into her mind, she immediately remembered how very unsafe things were right then.

She pulled gently out of the kiss, reluctantly blinking back into the room.

"Well, that's a good start to the day," Zach said with a grin, his arms still around her.

She smiled and nodded. "It definitely is."

"Okay," Zach said, taking a step back, which only made Ava want to take a step forward to close the gap again. He pulled out his phone and started typing, and while Ava was still trying to figure out what he was doing, her own phone started vibrating.

She hit the button to answer. "Am I supposed to say hello?" she asked, smirking.

"No, you don't have to talk. Go get ready like you normally would. Just don't go out of reach of the phone."

"Got it," Ava said, nodding, then headed to the door and straight out, turning only to wave her phone in Zach's direction, letting him know she would keep it by her side.

Outside, Ava scanned the area for threats. If Justin was out there and had a scope on her, there was little she could do. But not seeing anything obvious, she made her way back to her place, thinking about what she'd said to Zach.

She didn't know if what she said was true—about how Justin wouldn't do anything rash because he was still toying with her. Hell, she'd shot him, riled the bear, and frankly had no idea what he'd do now—Justin had never been known for being the calmest agent out there, but she didn't have a plan and needed time.

And in the meantime, she would keep a closer watch on this town than anyone ever had before.

Chapter 10

If Zach thought the bell over the door at The Other Apple Store had been bad before, it was absolutely driving him up the wall now. Never in his life had his senses been on such high alert, and he was suddenly suspicious of everyone, even people he'd known all his life. Which was ridiculous, but it wasn't like he could make the feelings go away.

And since it was the Apple Cider Festival, that damned bell kept chiming almost nonstop. A group of women would come in, and Zach would be suspicious of them, even though he knew Justin was a guy. A senior couple strolled in, and he'd be suspicious of them too. What if Justin had coconspirators of the geriatric variety? A family of four strolled in and Zach was especially suspicious…like seriously, why weren't those kids in school? Did we all just take our kids to random towns in the middle of the school year now? *Come on, people!*

The worst part was, he knew he was being ridiculous, but he couldn't help it. This thing with Ava was too important. He couldn't risk anything happening to it before it even got started. If they didn't see it through, he'd always wonder. And then his thoughts turned to the kiss

that morning. It had been so different from the one yesterday. Maybe there hadn't been as many sparks flying
as with the first one, but Zach kinda loved that. Because
he knew sometimes their life could be full of passion,
sometimes full of friendship, and sometimes simple appreciation and love. It was the perfect blend…much like
the perfect cup of coffee, he thought, as Ava walked up
and jolted him out of his daydream.

"Whatcha thinking about?" she asked.

"Um, nothing," Zach said, bringing the cup to his lips
a little too quickly and sloshing coffee over the edge of
the cup, thankfully missing his clothes by about a mil-
limeter.

"Yeah." Ava nodded. "I've been thinking a lot about,
um, nothing too," she said, and even shot him a wink
before she moved on to the next table.

Cripes, Zach thought. Here he was daydreaming when
he was supposed to be figuring out a plan to save the
love of his life.

*Wait. Love of his life? Was that what Ava was? No,
it was way too early to know for sure. Of course, when
does anyone ever know for sure, really?*

Damn it! He was doing it again.

He shook all thoughts out of his head and concentrated only on finding a plan. A way to find this guy. A
guy he didn't have even the slightest clue what he looked
like, what he sounded like…nothing. Zach's shoulders
slumped.

He'd never felt so helpless in his whole life.

The jingle of the bells above the door interrupted his
thoughts for the thirty-eight millionth time. A man, all
alone, which was suspicious for the festival. Most peo-

ple came with their family, or a group of friends, usually the ladies, or with someone who had newly become special to them. The Apple Cider Festival was nothing if not "the perfect weekend date destination," as the regional papers loved to tout.

Zach watched him closely. The man could have ducked into the coffee shop while his wife and kids were off bobbing for apple-themed prizes or perusing the local apple butters and honeys. Lord knew it was exactly what Zach would be doing if he was forced to attend some weird town's festival against his will.

But the man wasn't looking like he was having a crappy time. In fact, he looked downright cheerful, which Zach would have loved to say was strange, but in this town, cheer was basically the religion. The damn guy looked like he fit in perfectly, which was just so annoying. But Zach was used to pushing little annoyances out of the way, so he decided to give the guy the benefit of the doubt. Who knew, maybe the poor guy was just happy not to be stuck in some work cubicle for the day.

The man gave his order of coffee and an apple fritter—a little basic, but a solid order nonetheless—to Maureen, who was manning the counter while Ava no doubt created some delectable concoction in the back.

Zach pretended to be engrossed in his computer screen as the man sat, choosing the table directly across from him so they were facing each other.

Zach could never understand this move. Why, of all the places in a restaurant or café, would someone choose to sit staring straight at another human? Talk about awkward. He supposed some people did it on purpose, since they loved to chat with strangers…another thing he couldn't figure out. Ava would love it, Zach thought, then suddenly realized that could be a real benefit to him once they were officially together, since she could be the one to field all the awkward "people encounters."

Zach pretended to work for a while, keeping a keen eye on the stranger across from him, even though he'd pretty much decided the guy was harmless. Of course, it wouldn't hurt to know for sure, so he decided to take a sip of coffee, which he'd been avoiding since it would mean taking his eyes off his screen and potentially engaging with those around him, including the man in question. Which, if he was trying to glean any kind of information—like whether he was a cold-blooded, murderous spy—it would probably be the quickest and easiest way. Well, quickest, anyway. There was nothing easy about talking to strangers in Zach's book. He moved his cup to his lips and took a long sip, gazing all around until finally his eyes landed on the man.

"You look pretty deep in thought there," the man said the literal second Zach acknowledged his presence.

Zach had known it. The man had been waiting all along to talk to someone. Which Zach always thought of as kind of insulting, since it wasn't Zach this person was particularly interested in talking to—he could have been absolutely anyone in the world and this man would have been perfectly happy. Like, if you're perfectly fine talking with just anyone, it had to mean you really only wanted to hear yourself talk, right?

"Um, yeah, I guess so," Zach answered.

"Got a deadline?" the man continued. "I assume you must be a writer by trade if you're working that hard in the middle of a Wednesday," he said, grinning.

At least, Zach thought, it wasn't a goofy grin. The guy seemed like a normal guy.

"Uh, no deadline. Well, at least not yet," Zach answered. "Just kicking around a few ideas, seeing what they might turn into."

"Nice," the man said. "I used to write. Wasn't as good at it as I wanted to be, unfortunately."

Zach knew the feeling well. He was pretty sure every writer knew the feeling, really, and after the little nugget of common ground, he found he was the one who was suddenly asking questions. "What did you write?"

The man shrugged. "Nonfiction stuff mostly." He grinned. "The problem was the research. I hated the research. So much time spent feeling like you're not actually accomplishing anything even though you're laying the groundwork, or whatever."

Zach tilted his head back and forth in agreement. "Yeah, not my favorite either. Although there's still some research involved in fiction."

"Ah, fiction. Yes, that's true I suppose," the man said. "But it's not all research, all the time."

"So, were you a journalist then?" Zach asked, finding he was actually enjoying chatting with the guy.

"Educational books," he said. "And then creating online courses for schools after that."

"Interesting," Zach said. "Sounds like it would require a lot of—"

"Research," they both said at the same time, then shared a small chuckle.

"Nothing against the educational sector," the guy said, "but lately I've been craving something a bit more creative."

Zach nodded. "So what's next then?"

"Well, I don't know, to be honest. I've been toying with the idea of a novel."

"Also not easy work," Zach said, "but it is reward-ing...mostly."

"I bet," the guy said, a bit of a gleam in his eye now.

"Tell you what," Zach said. "Why don't you we ex-change numbers, and if you do decide to take that route, let me know. I'm happy to lend a hand where I can." Writing was such a solitary practice, and could be dis-couraging, especially when starting out. If he hadn't had the help of a few key people early on in his career, he never would have gotten to where he was. He liked to pay it forward whenever he got the chance...as long as it wasn't someone who seemed like they were going to take advantage. Which, by now, he could usually spot a mile away. But this guy seemed genuine enough.

"That's very generous of you," the man said, pulling out his phone.

Zach did the same and they exchanged electronic busi-ness cards. "'Glen Abrams,'" Zach said, reading the info aloud.

Glen nodded. "The listing has my previous educa-tional work info attached, but the number's still the same. This way, you'll have a better chance at remem-bering who I am down the road." He stood and moved closer to Zach's table, holding out his hand.

Zach stood and took it. "Perfect," he said.

"Well, I better get going," Glen said. "The wife's prob-ably out there figuring a way to convince me we need to move out to the country," he said. "Not that I don't love the country, but I think I'm more of a city guy."

"Fair enough," Zach said, thinking he wished there were a few more guys as down to earth as he was in this world.

Ava's stomach seized, her lunch threatening to make an encore appearance as she stood in the shadows watching Zach shake hands with the man who wanted to kill her.

Had tried to kill her and was back to finish the job.

The moment their hands touched, a lightning bolt of clarity shot through her.

What the hell was she doing?

Every moment…every second she stayed in town was another moment she was putting the people she cared about at risk.

How could she have been so careless? She should have been packing the moment she discovered she hadn't taken Justin out back at the Lawson house.

She knew Justin would try something else to mess with her—that he wanted nothing more than to make her suffer the way he must believe he'd been suffering for the past five years—but she didn't think he'd go after the people around her. Not the ones closest to her. Sure, he put people in danger with the water tower and the fire, but those were simply potential innocent casualties—something Justin never cared enough about.

But she was the Sparrow, trained not to get close to people. Trained to easily walk away the moment it was time. Trained to never let her feelings get in the way.

Of course, if Justin had been watching her for any length of time, a thought making her intensely queasy all over again, he would know she'd dropped that notion a long time ago. Longer than she was even willing to admit to herself.

Worse, it was the reason she was still in town when she should have been long gone.

And she'd bet her life Justin had known exactly what he was doing. He knew the moment the people who were really in her life were threatened—something that happened simply by being in the same room with Justin— she would have no choice but to leave.

He was smoking her right out of her town. Right out of her new life.

She wanted to drop everything and go, just turn around, walk right out the door of that kitchen and never look back. But that wasn't how the town of Ambrosia Falls worked. In about two minutes flat, someone would wonder where she'd gone. And about one minute later, someone would ask Zach if he'd seen her. And then he would come after her. She wouldn't even have a chance to pack the essentials—namely the supplies and weapons she had stashed in various corners of her house—before he'd be on her. Telling her she couldn't go. Telling her they were in this together. Telling her all the things that terrified her to her core.

Because they could not be in this together. Not really. Zach was a capable guy, but he wasn't trained like she was…or like Justin was. He wouldn't stand a chance out there. And she couldn't deal with him out there either. She'd be far more worried about protecting Zach than she'd ever be for herself. She didn't know what she'd do if something ever happened to Zach.

She could never live with herself.

A plan quickly formed in her head. She hated when

plans came so easily. The easy plans were usually only easy because there was a lack of options. And this time, she only had one option—run—and Justin knew it as well as she did.

The afternoon went by quickly. Too quickly.

Ava was going back and forth in her mind about how to say goodbye to Zach. Imagining not saying goodbye to him was inconceivable but telling him she was leaving was not a choice either. He'd try to talk her out of it, or worse, try to follow her.

The only thing she could do was sneak away in the night, being far more careful this time to make sure he wouldn't see her leave. When she'd first arrived in town all those years ago, she'd made several contingency plans, and she still had a beat-up old Chevy truck in storage across town. She'd have to pack up the things she needed and make her way there on foot. It wouldn't be easy, since she wanted at least a few days' worth of supplies, but she'd been in worse situations.

If luck were on her side, maybe Justin wouldn't catch on about her other mode of transport right away. He'd know she was gone in the morning—right along with everyone else in town and probably within a twenty-five-mile radius too—but half a day's head start might be the best she could do. Especially if Justin didn't know what she was driving or which direction she'd gone.

Still, she couldn't leave without saying something to Zach. She couldn't be that cruel.

Around the time Zach packed up his stuff and was heading out to get Chloe from school, the idea of a letter came to her. And if she left it in his mailbox, he wouldn't see it until he checked for the mail in the morning, or hopefully longer. It would be perfect. She'd be long gone, and he wouldn't have too much of a chance to worry.

Then, of course, her thoughts started churning over what to write. It wasn't like she could just be all like, thanks for everything, byeee! Ugh.

But how could you tell someone how much they meant to you in one little letter? She hoped he already knew—at least somewhat—how large a role in her life he'd come to play, but she was sure he didn't fully understand how much he meant to her. He couldn't understand that he was everything, and everything was something she'd never even come close to before.

She had closed herself off her entire life, even with Justin, she realized. Coming to Ambrosia Falls she'd seen how the real world could be—simple, even if it wasn't easy, and filled with a comfort she had never known before.

It was like the town—and Zach—had woken her from a hazy dream world and, for the first time in her life, filled everything with color.

After the rush of folks buying their breads and desserts to take home for dinner, Ava locked up the store the same way she did every evening. She didn't take anything extra with her—everything she would need was back at her place. Her supplies were mostly ready to go. She just needed to gather them all from their hiding places around her house, then slip out into the night. Fingers crossed she'd be unseen, by Justin and, most especially, by Zach.

She drove home and parked her car in the garage like she always did, then went into the house and texted Zach first thing.

Hey, I'm home, but I'm beat. It was an easy excuse, considering neither of them had gotten any sleep the night before. I've double-checked all the doors and windows and have the security system on. Gotta get some sleep. Have a good night.

Short, sweet, and just familiar enough he wouldn't get suspicious. Even though everything had changed between them in the past couple days, they'd never texted each other anything more intimate than the sort of message she'd just written, so she hoped it would work.

A minute later, her phone dinged with a text.

Me too. Please be careful. See you in the morning.

You be careful too, she typed, feeling a twinge of guilt at the see you in the morning part.

She avoided the letter writing as long as she could, going around the house and collecting only the essentials—small weapons she could easily carry, food supplies meant for backwoods camping, a couple changes of clothes and a second pair of sturdy shoes in case the whole thing went south, and she had to make her way on foot. The final things she packed were various forms of ID—with several different aliases—and some thick rolls of cash she'd been slowly adding to each week over the years.

And then it was time. She set her bag by the back door and sat down at her kitchen table with a pen and paper. She'd gone back and forth all day about what to write, finally deciding she owed it to Zach to lay it all out there. Not the stuff about her history or why Justin was so focused on her, but about the way she felt.

Dear Zach,

By the time you see this letter, I'll be gone. Long gone, I hope. But I couldn't leave without saying goodbye. I know I'm robbing you of your chance to say it back, and I'll forever be sorry for that, but I couldn't figure out any other way.

I had to go. I love you and Chloe too much to keep putting you in danger.

You might notice I used the word *love*. And I want you to know I don't mean it in the way you love your parents or your friends. Yes, you are my best friend, but I also want you to know I've been madly, head over heels in love with you for years. Maybe since the moment I laid eyes on you. The problem was, I didn't really know what love was. I'd never let myself have that before, and I guess I kind of thought I'd go the rest of my life without it.

I haven't told you everything about my past, but what you need to know is this: you were the reason I kept going. This interesting guy next door. The one who was so good with his kid, the one the whole town loved despite his efforts to push them all away, the one everyone knew they could count on. The one who made the days go by effortlessly, the one who gave me the inspiration for my recipes, the one who, without my even realizing it, was the reason I did everything I did.

Because that's who you are, Zach.

The one.

I thought love was something you *let* happen to you. I didn't know it could come along and hit you over the head, forever changing you whether you liked it or not. I was arrogant. I didn't think I could ever be touched by the big L word. But I was 100 percent wrong, and it's fine if you don't feel the same way back—in fact, I *hope* you don't, because leaving is going to be the hardest thing I've ever done and I do not want that for you.

I never want you to hurt. I never want Chloe to hurt.

Which is, of course, the very reason I have to go.

This whole town has stolen my heart, but the biggest chunk of it will always be set aside for you. Never change, Zach. Knowing your kind, incredible, grumpy self is still out there living, breathing, thriving, will be the only thing that continues to keep me going.

Kiss Chloe for me and please, do everything you can to live your best life.

With my love forever,
Ava

Ava didn't realize she was crying. She had to move. She had to keep the important people safe.

She decided to leave the letter in Zach's mailbox. With any luck he wouldn't think to check the box for a few days. The only tricky part would be getting it there without him noticing. Unfortunately, Zach liked to watch out his kitchen window. She knew this because she was also a watcher, and now that she thought about it, her watching was aimed way too often at Zach's house. She would sit several feet back from the window, so anyone glancing over wouldn't immediately see her, and watch him standing at that kitchen sink lost in thought.

But he wasn't there now.

It might be her only chance. Every part of her screamed to put it off, but she might not get another shot. She had to go now, before she lost her nerve.

She stuffed the letter in an envelope, scribbled his name on it, checked the window facing Zach's one more time and snuck quietly out her front door, stepping carefully to make as little noise on the gravel as possible. It had never bothered her that the mailboxes were all the way at the street before. It wasn't much of an inconvenience to walk the thirty or so steps to retrieve the mail, but in that moment, the distance seemed like miles.

She reminded herself to breathe as she moved. That was the thing about sneaking…your instinct was to hold your breath, which was, of course, the worse thing a person could do when trying to be quiet. Finally, she made it, pulling the mailbox open slowly. It squeaked a little, but she slipped the metal flap shut and turned back toward her house.

A few more steps and she'd be home free.

Which was precisely when the door to Zach's house burst open and he came flying down the stairs, a look of pure panic on his face.

"Zach?" she said, and as he ran toward her, the terrible empty feeling of having to leave morphed into something else. Something along the lines of nauseated terror. "What's wrong?"

"She's gone," he said, out of breath, jumpy and looking like he was on the verge of tears. "Chloe is gone."

Chapter 11

"Okay, let's not panic," Ava said, though it made it a hell of a lot harder for Zach not to panic when Ava looked like she was about to panic too.

His mind swirled. How could he have let this happen? He knew there was a dangerous person in town, and he hadn't even thought to make sure his daughter was by his side at all times? What was wrong with him? Sure, he'd grown up in this lazy small town his whole life and had literally never seen anything dangerous happen. There'd been some tragedies, of course. Accidents and weather-related catastrophes no one had seen coming. But the thought someone could do something to hurt the people of Ambrosia Falls on purpose...it didn't seem real.

Except he had known there was a threat. He should have been more vigilant.

Thought he had been, to be honest, though he supposed he didn't have it in him to think like a bad dude and had been so focused on keeping Ava safe he would never, in a million years, have thought Chloe was in danger.

"Let's get inside," Ava said, glancing around in a way Zach did not like.

He couldn't give two shits about his own well-being, but at least had the presence of mind to know he couldn't help Chloe if he became incapacitated somehow, so he let Ava lead him up his front steps and into the house.

"Are you certain she's gone?" Ava asked, guiding Zach to a kitchen chair. "Like, does she have any hiding places or anything?"

Zach shook his head. "She's never really been a hiding kind of kid."

Ava started to pace. "What about friends? Would she sneak out to go see anyone, do you think? Was she mad about anything?"

"Mad?" Zach asked, putting his elbows on the table and leaning his head in his hands. He was having trouble catching any of the thoughts pummeling through his head.

"Like, did you guys get in a fight or anything?"

He looked up from his hands. "What? No. We weren't fighting. We had a normal dinner, the same as we do every day, and then she went upstairs to finish some homework. She was working on some big project for science class or something."

"So, she was up there for a while," Ava said.

Zach nodded. "At least I thought she was." He put his head back in his hands. "Oh God," he said, his voice strangled.

"Did you hear anything during the time she was up there?"

Zach shook his head. "Nothing. Which maybe should have clued me in? But I thought she was sitting at the desk in her room working. It's not like she would normally be roaming around or anything. And then I went to check on her and she was just…gone…" he said, his voice trailing off.

"Okay, so is it possible she could have simply come downstairs and headed out without you knowing?"

"She's never done anything like that before," Zach said. "I mean, she walks to her friends' houses all the time, and to Mom's, but she's always told me where she was going."

"Maybe she forgot this time," Ava said, and Zach could tell the hope in her voice was false, even if it did inject a tiny spurt of it into him too.

"I guess. I mean, it would be the world's worst timed coincidence, considering all the other stuff going on around town and what's going on with…you," he said, not sure how else to say what he was thinking.

That this was no coincidence at all.

"I agree," Ava said, "but we have to cover all our bases, right? It's the smart thing to do."

"I have to get out there. Start searching," Zach said, getting up from the table and starting to pace along with Ava.

"But," Ava said quietly, "search where?"

Zach stopped midstep. It hadn't occurred to him it might be pointless to rush out of the house and start randomly driving around. Where would he go? What would he do? And now that it was dark out, how would that even work? "Well, I have to do something," he said, trying to keep the anger out of his voice, though it wasn't working.

"I think we should at least call around to make sure she hasn't gone to a friend's house or your mom's or something before we jump to conclusions. I agree the timing is terrible, and we have to consider all the possibilities, but this is at least a place to start."

Zach swallowed hard, not liking any of it one bit. But he didn't have any other ideas. At least not any rational ones.

"So let's call around and see if anyone knows where she is. Just casually, you know, so more people don't get freaked out," Ava said. "Because if this is who we think it might be, we're going to want to keep this as simple as possible. We can't have all the people in town freaking out and getting in the way if we need to move to a plan B."

"Yeah, okay," Zach said.

At least it was something to do. There was absolutely no way he could do nothing. He just wasn't sure how he was supposed to keep the fear out of his voice as he called around.

An hour later Zach's panic was going into full-blown freak-out mode. No one had seen Chloe. Deep down, he'd known all along they wouldn't get anywhere with the calls, but they had to try.

"At least we managed not to freak anyone out, I guess," he said.

"I'm so sorry, Zach," Ava said, her eyes red as much from emotion as from exhaustion.

"It's not your fault," Zach said.

He wanted to be angry at Ava. To be mad she ever came to this town and put all of them in this position, though of course he couldn't be. She had been a victim in all this as much as anyone. More than anyone. She was the innocent bystander who did nothing besides being in the wrong place at the wrong time and getting involved with the wrong dude. And Zach knew a little something about getting involved with the wrong person. A person who turned out not to be who he thought they were at all, so he could hardly get mad at Ava for doing the same thing.

"This is definitely my fault," Ava said, a tear falling.

She looked like she was about to crumple, but Zach couldn't let that happen. He needed her to keep it together. Because if Ava fell apart, there was no way he wasn't going to follow.

"Nope," he said, putting his arms around her and pulling her close. "First of all, this isn't your fault. This is all shit you had no control over. You are not putting all this on yourself. And second, you simply can't go down that rabbit hole because I need you to keep me calm. If we both lose it, we have no chance. We have to keep it together for Chloe."

Ava pulled in a deep breath and nodded. "You're right. I'm just going to put all these feelings aside and deal with them later."

"Yup, we will deal with them later," he said. "Okay, so what's next?" he asked, as they broke apart from the hug.

"I'm not sure what we can do before the sun comes up," Ava said, making panic flash though Zach's eyes again. She put her hands up. "I'm not saying we're going to do nothing—I'm just saying things are going to be limited."

"I'm not going to sit here all night," Zach said.

"I know. I'm going to go upstairs and check Chloe's room, see if there are any clues there."

"Right, okay. I'll go check outside, under the window of her room—see if there's anything there," he said, heading for the door.

But before he got two steps out of the house, something stopped him cold.

An envelope—bright white contrasting against the dark porch floor.

"Ava," he called before she got too far away. "I think I found something."

This was 100 percent her fault. It killed her to keep the real her a secret from Zach, especially with everything going on, but she couldn't come clean now. If she did, Zach would hate her, which she could live with, but she couldn't live with anything happening to Chloe. She needed Zach to trust her, to work with her, for their best chance at getting Chloe back.

She was halfway up the stairs when he called to her, his hands shaking as he turned toward her with an envelope in his hands.

Ava's stomach seized.

Zach came back into the house in a daze, shutting the door absently.

"Do you want me to open it?" Ava asked.

She wanted to be the one to handle whatever was going to be inside that envelope. She was trained to preserve evidence, to keep her cool no matter what the contents might be. But Chloe was Zach's daughter, and she had no right to be the first to see, even if this was about her in the end. Right now, all that mattered was Chloe. And Zach.

Ava cringed as Zach ripped into the envelope, thinking about all the things that could happen. There could be a dangerous substance, or worse, some kind of explosive even though the envelope appeared to be flat from where she stood.

Zach pulled a photo from the envelope, and Ava rushed over, praying it would be proof of life and not something much, much worse.

She let out a breath when Chloe's scared, but very much alive face looked back from yet another instant camera print.

"It's proof of life," Ava said quickly. "It means she's okay."

"Okay?" Zach said, his voice hitching. "She's tied up. There's a gag in her mouth."

"I know. And that's obviously bad, but it's not Chloe he wants."

"She looks so scared," Zach said, running his finger along Chloe's face in the picture.

"We're going to get to her," Ava said. "We just need to find out where he's keeping her, and I'll surrender. He'll hand Chloe to you and this will all be over. Easy peasy," Ava said.

"That is not easy peasy," Zach said, an angry edge to his voice. "I'm not going to hand you over to this guy."

"It's the best option, Zach," Ava said, and she meant it.

She would do anything to save Chloe, and if that meant the end of herself, so be it.

"I don't care about easy," Zach said. "I care about getting Chloe back *and* keeping you safe."

Ava waved away his comment. "Whatever, either way we need to figure out where this is," she said, poking at the photo, "and get to her."

Zach flipped the picture over. *Don't even think about the cops, Sparrow.*

"Sparrow?"

"It's, uh, what he used to call me," she said, hoping he wouldn't ask too many questions.

"This guy is getting weirder and weirder," Zach said. "Although he clearly didn't do his research if he thinks cops are going to be a problem around here."

Ava took the picture from Zach to study it closer, starting to pace, hoping it would help her think.

"If he wants you to come and find her," he asked, "why doesn't he just tell us where she is? You'd think he'd have had plenty of time to set up traps for us or whatever."

Ava shrugged one shoulder. "That's not how Justin works. He only feels powerful when he's playing people. When he's messing with their minds."

"Is that what he's doing to Chloe?" Zach asked, with something wild behind his eyes.

Ava shook her head quickly. "I don't think he'll hurt her. Not if we do what he says. I mean, I don't think it's impossible, but Chloe isn't who he's after. He's doing this to hurt me."

"Okay, I get that, but how in the hell are we supposed to find her from this?" Zach asked, pulling the photo right out of Ava's hand, which, given the circumstances, Ava wasn't going to fight him on, no matter how much she needed to study it and hope for a clue.

"He must think we'll be able to figure it out somehow," she said.

Suddenly Zach stopped. "This was taken in the daylight."

Ava moved beside him, close enough so they could both see. "Right, I didn't even think of that. So if she was still here for dinner, that doesn't leave much of a time frame for it to still be light out. What time did you eat?"

"It was late. I cooked a roast, which always takes a while, but it's Chloe's favorite."

"So we're looking at a window of like, two hours, tops."

"Which means she can't be far, right?" Zach said, a tiny sliver of hope trickling into his voice.

"Yeah, if he got her to this…whatever this is," Ava said, motioning to the photo, "and then came back here again so quickly, it was only about an hour that we were making calls before we found the envelope."

"Jesus," Zach said, running his fingers hard through his hair. "I just realized this asshole was right here. We could have had him." Zach raced back to the front door and whipped it open.

Ava wasn't sure if he was expecting to find Justin right there on his doorstep, or what, but she knew he was long gone. Justin didn't take chances. He likely would have waited until he had a full view of the two of them to risk creeping up to the door. He was good at what he did. Damn good.

Ava just hoped she was still better.

Zach shut the door again and threw out a string of curses that would make a sailor blush.

"We should try to get some sleep," Ava said.

At a time like this, it was unlikely to happen, but she knew from experience sleep would make everything so much easier and the likelihood of success much greater. "We can head out as soon as the sun starts coming up."

Zach flopped onto the couch and let out a half-hearted chuckle. "I can't see how there's any way I could sleep knowing Chloe is out there, scared and alone."

"I know," Ava said, "but we should try anyway. We'll be better for helping Chloe that way."

"We don't even know where we're going," Zach said.

"We'll figure it out."

"How though? We have no idea where to start." He held up the photo of Chloe. "This could be pretty much anywhere."

"We'll find her," Ava said, with as much confidence as she could muster.

"You don't know that. You can't know that," Zach said, a hint of anger breaking through the fear in his voice.

"I do know it," Ava said. "Because I know you, and I know me. And we aren't going to stop until we do."

Zach slumped his shoulders and nodded. Ava knew his mind would be reeling all night. She glanced at her watch. It was about five hours until the sun came up again.

And it would be the longest five hours of their lives.

Chapter 12

Zach knew he needed sleep but knowing that didn't get him any closer to actually getting any. Still, he tried to rest as much as possible as he studied the photo of Chloe. He could hardly stand to look at it, almost relieved she was gazing slightly away from the camera—he wasn't sure he'd be able to take seeing her fear head-on. Which made him feel like a coward, but his heart was already ripping in two catching even a glimpse of her.

He hoped Chloe would be able to sleep…at least she'd get a bit of a break if she did. She had to know he was coming for her, right? He hoped it would be enough to keep her spirits up, to stay strong and positive. A tiny smile played at the edge of his lips. He would bet his life Chloe was giving this Justin jackass a piece of her mind. Maybe that's why she had the cloth around her mouth. Chloe was a fierce, determined kid and would likely not be making it easy on the guy.

Of course, that realization terrified Zach, and he sent a silent plea out to the universe to keep her safe. He couldn't lose her.

He just couldn't.

Zach leaned his head back and closed his eyes, picturing Chloe's sweet face laughing at the dinner table. She'd been humoring him after he'd told a particularly bad joke about a snowman and "the Winternet," and she'd played right along even though she was way too old for the joke. She was so good at that. The bad dad jokes were kind of their thing. Sure, she—rightly—made fun of him over it, but she never told him to stop, even when her friends were around. And yeah, she might roll her eyes every now and then, but that was part of her charm. And part of what made it so fun to tell the stinkin' jokes in the first place.

He let out a heavy sigh as a tear escaped his eye, rolling down his cheek and toward his ear, but he couldn't be bothered to wipe it away. It didn't matter. Nothing mattered except finding Chloe.

Chloe, Chloe, Chloe. He had to find her…

Should they start with places close to town? She couldn't be more than two hours away, given the time frame they'd worked out earlier. Maybe they should start at the far end of that window—drive an hour out of town and work their way in? But which direction? And more importantly, how much ground could they cover before the sun went down again?

Zach's eyes snapped open.

"Hey," Ava said. Somehow, she was sitting in the chair across from him even though he hadn't heard her sit down. "You've been out for a few hours."

"I have?" Zach asked, then wiped a bit of drool from the corner of his mouth. "It didn't feel like I slept. The last thing I was thinking about was how much ground we can cover before sunset and then…"

A jolt went through Zach. "Where's the picture of Chloe?" he asked, a note of desperation in his voice.

Ava leaned over and grabbed it off the coffee table, holding it out to him.

He plucked it out of her hand and studied it. But this time he didn't look directly at Chloe. He looked past her, above her head to the window. It was how they'd known it was still daylight when the picture was taken. There it was.

"Look at this," Zach said, pointing to the direction the light shone in through the window. "The sun's coming in from this direction," he said, motioning to the area out past the left perimeter of the photo.

Ava let out a little gasp. "And we know the sun had to be close to setting when he took the picture."

"And the sun sets in the west...so this has to be west." He made the motioning gesture again.

"Which means this is north, east and south," Ava said, pointing to each edge of the photo as she said the directions.

"Which means this picture was taken somewhere south of town."

"Holy shit," Ava said.

Suddenly they were getting somewhere, Zach thought. "It's mostly woods out that way, which would make sense. I haven't gone hunting in years," he said. "Never liked the idea of shooting living things, you know? But I used to go with my dad when I was a kid. I think there are still a few hunting shacks out there."

"That's exactly what this looks like," Ava said, pointing at Chloe again. "It's small, likely one room, but has an area for a cot here and I'm assuming a bit of living quarters behind the photographer."

Zach knew Ava was avoiding saying kidnapper so he wouldn't get all worked up again, but avoiding it only served to bring it straight back to the forefront of his mind. "We need to get out there," he said, getting up.

"The sun will start coming up in about an hour. We can gather supplies, and by the time we're ready to leave, it will be close to rising."

"Sounds good," Zach said, heading upstairs to get changed. Ava headed toward the front door. "Wait, where are you going?"

"Home. To change and get ready," she said, pointing toward the door.

"I don't think we should split up. I can change quickly, then we can head to your place where I can stand watch while you get ready."

Ava raised her eyebrows and opened her mouth as if she were about to argue but must have thought better of it. "Sure, sounds good," she said. "I'll go see what you have for food and water."

Zach nodded and continued up the stairs to put on a few layers. In his experience, the woods could be either way too hot or way too chilly depending on the time of day and the direction of the sun. He tried to think of every possible scenario and couldn't help but feel underprepared for all of them.

He headed back downstairs and fished in the closet for his hiking boots he used occasionally when he and Chloe decided it was time to get outside and see some nature.

Ava handed him a couple bottles of water and kept

two for herself. "I'm pretty sure I don't have any of these at my place," she said, heading for the door.

Zach grabbed his keys and followed, letting her lead the way over to her place.

As they walked, Zach was on high alert. With the lights from their houses, they'd be sitting ducks if someone decided to shoot from out of the darkness. He strained to hear any noise that might be out of place but could barely think over the sound of the crickets. Had they always been that loud? A friggin' elephant could charge past and barely be heard over the damn things.

But in a few steps, they'd made it to Ava's and Zach was safely closing the door behind them.

Ava went toward the back door to her house and re-trieved a large backpack.

"Were you planning on going somewhere?" Zach asked.

Ava looked momentarily surprised, then gave him a little smile. "I learned a long time ago it's good to be prepared, that's all," she said with a shrug.

But Zach had been in her house dozens of times, and there had definitely not been an already packed bag lean-ing up against the back door. "Jesus," he said, rubbing his face. "You were going to leave."

Ava pulled in a long breath. "It's the only way, Zach. And this…what happened to Chloe only proves it. As soon as we find her, I'm either going to have to go with Justin, or if we get very lucky, I'll make it out too and can get a head start on him."

"You can't leave," Zach said.

Ava stood in front of him and looked him straight in the eye. "Except I have to."

Zach shook his head.

"We can't waste time arguing about it," Ava told him. "I have a second gun at the store. We should stop by and grab it before we head out."

"Why do you have even one gun?" Zach asked, but Ava just gave him a look.

Of course, he knew the answer. The guy who now had his daughter. It was going to take a while to rearrange the ideas he'd had of Ava's life before Ambrosia Falls into the truth he now knew. Trying to picture her under the influence of this guy, helpless and desperate, didn't compute with anything he knew about her. She'd always been so confident, so strong. He couldn't reconcile any other thoughts of her, no matter how hard he tried. And the way she was checking and double-checking her gear, which included doing a safety and ammo check on her handgun, did not make the visual of a helpless Ava any easier to grasp onto.

"How much gas do you have? Your truck will do better out on the rougher roads," Ava said, zipping her backpack with finality.

"Yeah, we should be good. Filled up a couple days ago."

"Great, let's go," Ava said, and Zach marveled at her businesslike tone.

Like she was a completely different person. Except, she wasn't a completely different person. This was just another side of her. A side that, even though it was jarring, made a hell of a lot more sense than some damsel in distress scenario.

A few minutes later they pulled up to the coffee shop, both jumping out of the vehicle. Zach was not about to leave Ava by herself for even a second. He didn't know what this Justin guy was capable of, but he was not going to make the mistake of underestimating him.

Zach thought he had been prepared for anything, but as he went to close the truck door, the silence-shattering siren and the red and blue lights bursting out of nowhere definitely caught him a teensy bit off guard.

And like a damn fool, he promptly stuck up his hands.

Zach was not good at attempting to look innocent.

It was a good thing the guy was a writer, because he would certainly not make it as an actor, or you know, any profession requiring even the slightest hint of faking anything, anywhere, at any time.

"You okay there, man?" the officer said as he stepped out of his vehicle.

Ava shot Zach a look that she hoped conveyed he needed to lower his arms, and she hoped the officer wouldn't pick up on it in the early morning light.

"Oh, uh, yeah, sorry," Zach said sheepishly, lowering his arms. "You, uh, startled me a bit."

The officer nodded. "Yeah, sorry about that. I like to see how people react. Tells me a lot."

"Does it?" Zach asked politely, not doing a very good job at hiding the panic on his face.

"Is there anything we can do to help you out, Officer?" Ava quickly interjected, desperate to take the focus off Zach so he could hopefully regain some semblance of composure.

"Y'all are up a little early, aren't you?" the man asked.

Ava shrugged one shoulder. "I'm always up this early," she said. "Bakery owner." She motioned to the store.

"Ah," the officer said, raising an eyebrow. "Looks like a nice store. Was thinking I might have to come in for a coffee when you open."

"We'd love to have you," Ava said, turning on her small-town charm.

Which was strange. She'd settled into the small-town charm persona so fully over the last couple years it became who she was, except...she realized now she'd been in a different mode ever since she learned about Justin's reappearance.

Sparrow mode.

"And you?" the officer said, turning back to Zach.

"Oh, uh, just helping out a bit," he said. "You know, the Apple Cider Festival and all."

"You help with the baking," the officer said, a sarcastic lilt to his voice.

Zach's brows furrowed together, and Ava held her breath, terrified he was going to say something even more suspicious, but he simply said, "Of course," effectively conveying he couldn't understand why that would be strange at all and putting the sexism right back in its place.

"Got a lot of gear in there for a coffee shop," the officer said, flicking on a light and shining it into the second-row seat of the truck.

"Yeah," Zach said, "we were out hiking yesterday. I was a little tired afterward, and I guess I got lazy about putting our stuff away."

The guy nodded and took a step back. Ava got the feeling he decided they were harmless. "I hear there's been some trouble up this way," the officer said. "You guys know anything about that?"

"Sure," Ava said, jumping in. "Who doesn't? The water tower. The fire at the baking competition stage. Gotta say, I'm pretty bummed about that one." She leaned in close to the man. "I usually make a pretty good showing."

"I bet you do, what with being the town baker and all," the officer said, giving her a courtesy smile. "But you don't have any insight beyond the basics? No ideas as to how any of it happened?"

"Oh," Ava said, doing her best to look surprised, "unfortunately no. It's all just so…strange."

"And you?" he said, turning to Zach.

Zach shrugged, and it only looked a little forced. "No idea. Nothing like it has ever happened around here before."

"You lived here long?"

"All my life," Zach said.

The officer nodded, looking Zach up and down, making him squirm all over again.

"I'm sorry," Ava said. "I wish we could help, but if there's nothing else, I really do need to get started on my day."

"Right, no problem," the officer said, pulling a card out. "I'll be nosing around town a bit today, so if anything else out of the ordinary happens, I'd appreciate it if y'all could let me know."

"Sure thing—" Ava took the card and peered at the name "—Officer Banyan," she said, shooting him her best "no need to worry about me, I'm just an innocent baker" smile.

He tipped his hat and got in his car, backing away as Ava and Zach went into The Other Apple Store.

"Holy shit," Zach said, the moment they were safely inside. "What the hell do we do now?"

"We're going to have to make it look like we're doing exactly what we said we'd be doing. I figure there's another hour before the town starts coming to life and he'll have other things to be focused on. We can't risk moving your truck right away. I say we wait it out for a bit, then you calmly head out by yourself—it'll look like I'm staying here—make sure the coast is clear, then come around back and pick me up."

"I don't know if I can wait an hour," Zach said, starting to pace.

"If you're going to look all nervous and guilty, can you at least come back to the kitchen and do it?" Ava asked, pulling him toward the kitchen doors. "Officer Banyan is probably looking at us right now."

Zach let out a groan. "I am so bad at this," he said as they moved to the back.

"Not that bad," Ava said. "There were moments out there I almost believed you."

Zach rolled his eyes. "Almost? Great. I wonder what I looked like to a trained professional."

As a trained professional, Ava thought he'd done okay. Unfortunately, she couldn't exactly explain that to him.

"Jesus. Of all the times for the cops to show up," Zach said, able to pace freely now that they were out of view.

"I know, but I think we're fine. This might be better, anyway. Maureen will be here right around the time it should be safe for us to go. I'll tell her I have a migraine or something and ask if she can run the store for the day. I was planning on closing, but this will be better. It'll keep the town gossip down a bit."

Zach nodded. "Okay, yeah, you're probably right. But how in the hell are we going to kill this hour? I'm dying here. I have to do something."

"Easy," Ava said. "If the store is opening today, we have to get some baking done."

Zach looked as terrified as she'd ever seen him. Which, given the past several hours, was saying something.

"It's fine," she said. "I'll find you some easy stuff to do."

An hour later the place was full of baking smells and Zach still looked just as nervous. Ava couldn't fault the guy—he was hardly in an ideal mindset to be learning the ropes of a bakery, especially given that it had been a while since he'd had a proper sleep.

While he was watching over the mixer, adding dry ingredients a small amount at a time, Ava took a moment to retrieve the gun she had hidden in the back closet on the top shelf behind a box of old marketing materials. She wished she could go down into the crawlspace and really arm up, but that might be a little hard to explain to Zach.

When she got back to the kitchen, Maureen had arrived and was grilling Zach about why he was there.

He seemed to be doing about as good a job at improv with Maureen as he had with good ole Officer Banyan.

"I'm helping a bit. Ava's, um, not feeling well," he said, swallowing guiltily.

"Hey, Maureen, I'm so glad you're here," Ava said, trying to look exhausted.

Which, she had to admit, wasn't much of a stretch.

"I woke up with a migraine this morning," she continued. "As you can see, I roped Zach into helping. Is there any way you can run the store today?"

Maureen looked from Ava to Zach, then back to Ava again. "So you called Zach? That seems a little weird. Unless you already knew he was up or—" Her eyes grew wide.

At first Ava wasn't sure what Maureen had figured out, panicking that somehow she knew about Chloe. About Justin. About all of it.

And then Maureen smirked. One of those knowing smirks that said loud and clear she knew you were up to something, and she knew exactly what that something was, wink, wink. And then her expression changed to something akin to pure glee. "Sure. Yeah definitely. I can run the store today," she said, then added a quick, "It's about time," with a happy sigh.

Oh, jeez, Ava thought. *This'll be flying through town faster than wildfire once the store opens.*

It was taking a little longer for Zach to catch on to what was going on. "What's about time?" he asked.

"Nothing," Ava said, grabbing his arm and leading him toward the door. "Would you mind giving me a ride home? Maybe grab your truck and come around back to pick me up?" Ava said, lifting her eyebrows with a look that said, *Just go, I'll deal with this.*

"Yeah, sure," Zach said, still a little dazed as she pushed him out of the kitchen.

"Omigod, spill!" Maureen said the second Zach was out of earshot.

Ava groaned. "Maureen, it's nothing. It's not what you think."

"Mmm-hmm," she said, not believing it for a second.

Ava wished a secret affair was the only thing she'd be dealing with over the next few hours, but she supposed a little rumor was the least of her worries, even though it was…embarrassing somehow. Not that Zach would be embarrassing to be with—definitely not—but the fact the whole town was going to go nuts over the whole thing, all thinking like they knew better way before either of them did. And yeah, that might actually be true, but they didn't know the half of what had been holding them back from exploring the possibilities.

She sighed as she stepped out the back door of her shop. Zach was already waiting, looking tired, worried and so heartbreakingly handsome behind the wheel of his truck. If only there was a chance to properly explore those possibilities someday.

"She thinks there's something going on between us, doesn't she," Zach said, looking like he both wanted to kick himself for not figuring it out sooner, and like he wanted to crawl under the nearest rock and hide for a very long time.

"She does," Ava said, staring straight ahead.

"This is not good," Zach said. "The whole town is going to be talking."

Ava waved the comment away. "It'll be okay. In fact, it might be good. It will keep everybody distracted, at least for today. We'll have time to get to Chloe, I can get out of town, Justin will follow and forget Ambrosia Falls even exists and everything will be fine."

"How would any of that be fine?" he asked, his eyes wild.

"I'm sorry you'll have to deal with the fallout of all

the gossip, but after I'm gone for a few days, everyone will forget all about it."

"That is not happening," Zach said.

"Zach, it's the only way. You know it's the only way."

"I absolutely do *not* know that it's the only way. And yeah, I'm good with focusing on Chloe for step one, but I'm not okay with you being bait for this guy to hurt yet another person I care about."

"You need to stop," Ava said.

"Stop what?"

"Caring about me. It's just not going to work."

"You and me won't work?" Zach said.

"Exactly."

He let out a hard breath. "Fine," he said, though he looked hurt. "That's not even what I'm worried about. And I'm not worried about any ridiculous gossip fallout either. This is about you being safe. Whether our friendship could ever become something else doesn't matter right now. What matters is the friendship itself, and frankly I'm pissed you're treating it like it's nothing."

"I know it's not nothing, Zach," Ava said, turning away, focusing on the passing landscape. "It's everything," she whispered.

Silence fell in the truck for the next several minutes.

Finally, Ava spoke. "Let's focus on Chloe. Nothing else matters if we don't get this next step right, okay?"

"I know, but…we're going to try to get this guy, right?"

Ava nodded. "In an ideal world, yes. But we can't assume we'll get close enough. And you said yourself you don't like the idea of hurting things. You won't even hunt, Zach."

"Innocent animals hunted for sport are very different from someone who is trying to kill the people I love."

Love.

Ava let that sit there, not knowing what to say in return. Especially since she wanted to scream at the top of her lungs that she loved him too.

"Just focus on Chloe," she eventually said instead.

Zach nodded. "Focus on Chloe."

And then I'm gone.

Chapter 13

"I think we're a few miles out from the first shack," Zach said after they'd driven for more than an hour.

"We shouldn't get too close," Ava said. "He'll hear us coming from miles away if we pull up in a one-ton truck."

Zach pulled to the side of the road. "Do we try to hide the truck?"

Ava looked around. "If you can find a place, it might help."

"There was a trail about a half mile back," he said. "We could go a little way down there."

"Yeah, that would be better," Ava said, her eyes scanning as much of the terrain as she could see, which wasn't much considering they'd been on a forest road for the past fifteen minutes. "Will we be coming back to the truck after we check out the first shack? Or going on foot?"

"If I remember correctly, this road ends not too much farther from here. I think we're on foot from here on out."

Ava nodded. "Carrying packs is going to make it harder, but we'll have to suck it up. How many shacks are there?"

"Only three I know of, but that doesn't mean there aren't more. Like I said, this isn't really my world."

"Fair enough. With any luck, there will be trails leading to any shacks you don't know about."

They heaved their packs over their shoulders and headed out. Ava followed Zach since he knew the terrain better than she did.

After hiking in silence for about twenty minutes, Zach held up his fist military-style to alert Ava to stop. They moved much slower then, and as silently as possible, though Ava couldn't help but feel like Zach could use a little more training in being stealthy. Or you know, any at all.

Zach ducked behind a tree, and Ava followed his lead, easing behind another where she had a good view of both Zach and the tiny cabin in the distance.

"Okay, so how are we going to play this?" Zach asked.

He had imagined a scenario where he'd quietly charge forward, gun in hand and eyes darting, scanning for potential targets. And he had to admit, that's pretty much the way the whole thing went down, except he was still back behind the tree thinking it all through while Ava whisper-yelled, "Follow me," and then moved out exactly the way he'd envisioned himself doing it.

He had no choice but to follow, watching Ava aim her handgun steadily in one direction and then the other, stepping lightly but quickly, nearly silent on her feet, moving closer and closer to the shack.

One thought kept repeating in his mind. *How is she so good at this?*

She paused at one last tree, pointed in the direction she was about to go. She motioned for him to move in the opposite direction, which he did, the adrenaline pumping.

Even though Ava had the longer route, she somehow made her way around the shack first, seamlessly ducking under the single window in the back, then moving around to the front. While all this was going on, Zach felt like a lumbering bear as he made his way much more loudly around the closer side of the shack, thankfully not having any windows to avoid, and got around to the front in time to watch Ava take her last couple steps toward the door, lunge back, then kick her leg near the handle of the door. With wood splinters raining, the door burst open, and Ava stepped inside, pointing her gun first to the right, and then immediately to the left as Zach finally bumbled in after her like some kind of clueless old-timey deputy.

"Clear!" Ava yelled, as if she'd done it a hundred times before.

Jesus.

"Um, okay," Zach said, standing there blinking, his mind moving in all kinds of directions.

He was upset and pissed that Chloe wasn't there. He wanted all this to be over. He wanted to know the people he loved were safe.

And he also wondered how in the fiery depths of hell Ava was so calm under pressure, seemed to know how to expertly handle a weapon, not to mention maneuver like some kind of tactical genius.

"Um, what was that?"

Ava turned to him. "What do you mean?"

"That," he said, waving his arm in a circular gesture. "Like the whole…rushing in like you're some kind of navy SEAL or something."

It was Ava's turn to stare and blink for a moment. "Um, I guess I was copying people on the TV," she said, shrugging. "Did it look ridiculous? It probably looked ridiculous. I'm sorry, that's so embarrassing. I guess I…kind of got caught up in the moment or something."

Zach squinted at her. "No. No, it looked very believable," he said. "Like, weirdly believable."

"Huh," Ava said, nodding slowly. "Okay then, um, that's good I guess."

They stood for a moment, then Ava spoke again. "Well, this clearly isn't the shack in the picture—the view out the window isn't the same at all so, we should get going."

"Right," Zach said, hiking his pack a little higher on his shoulders. "There's one a little farther toward Aspen Hill."

"Great," Ava said, "lead the way."

Thirty minutes or so later they slowed again, hiding in the trees several dozen yards from the shack Zach led them to.

"I have a feeling this could be the one," he said.

Ava nodded, working her jaw. "Okay, let's take it slow…be extra cautious."

Zach was still nodding when Ava was on the move again. *Shit.* He hurried after her, trying to be as quiet as possible, but it seemed to be one of those situations where the harder you tried at something, the worse you were at it.

He pulled in a deep breath, letting it out slowly through his mouth, trying to calm his racing heart, but by the time they neared the shack, he was breathing like he'd just run up ten flights of stairs.

Like the last time, they paused to get their bearings.

And that's when Zach saw it. A small, red shoe. Exactly like a pair of Chloe's.

Saliva filled his mouth as his stomach performed an impressive reenactment of one of those spinning teacup rides.

Strange that the man would have the presence of mind to grab shoes for her as he somehow stole Chloe out of her second-story bedroom window. The planning and precision it would have taken was enormous. Sure, Chloe's bedroom window looked out onto the forested edge of town, so it wasn't likely he'd be seen, but he had to be quiet enough that Zach wasn't alerted, and with a kid like Chloe, that couldn't have been easy. To think of him gathering up shoes on top of it all was wild. Like the man had thought of everything, including precisely how to execute his plan.

It was not a thought that comforted Zach.

Ava was signaling to get his attention. She'd seen the shoe too. This was definitely the place. She put her finger over her lips to signal silence, then began to move. They followed the same procedure as at the last shack, though now that Zach knew what to expect, he was able to round the front of the building at the same time as Ava.

Still, she was the one who got to the door first and gave it a kick that might have been even more intense than the one at the last shack. She whipped her gun right, then left, then once again…and to Zach's horror, yelled "Clear!"

"What do you mean, clear?" Zach asked, rushing inside, his eyes frantically covering every inch of the room. "She was here. This has to be the place. Look at the window, it's the same as in the photo." He dug into the side pocket of his cargo pants to retrieve the photo even though he already knew he was right. "Her shoe is outside. She has to be here."

* * *

Ava's heart sank, though she knew what she was feeling was nothing compared to what Zach must be feeling. Justin was an absolute bastard for putting them through all this. Not to mention what Chloe must be dealing with. She must be so scared. All alone with that jackass of a human who probably didn't know the first thing about kids. Ava could only hope he was feeding her decently and keeping her warm.

The silver lining was, she didn't think Justin would actually hurt Chloe...not yet, anyway. None of this was even about Chloe. It was about Ava, and Ava alone. Chloe was just another ploy. Another way to toy with her, to make her pay for finding him out and escaping all those years ago.

Zach started rummaging through some of the stuff in the cabin, lifting relatively recent food containers from the small counter, then throwing them back down again in disgust. He moved over to the bed and lifted the pillow, which was when Ava heard it.

A quiet, almost imperceptible high-pitched squeal. A squeal Ava had heard only once before...five years ago.

"Get out!" she yelled, yanking the back of Zach's shirt with more might than she knew she was capable of, and dove for the doorway, dragging Zach behind her.

He didn't question—didn't have time to question—following her lead as she turned and dove through the doorway as the first boom sounded, then a second... pieces of the shack exploding in every direction. Wood splinters shot through the air, then rained on them as Ava covered her head with her arms, hoping nothing more substantial was on its way down.

Since the shack didn't have much to it, the raining debris didn't take long to clear. Ava rolled onto her back to survey the damage. Her first thought was that the thing had been obliterated so fully that, if there hadn't been a black mark of ash where the shack once stood, no one would have known anything ever stood there at all. Her second thought was to wonder where the hell all the blood was coming from.

"Shit, Zach," she said, scrambling over to him.

He was breathing and conscious, but clearly in a lot of pain. The blood was pouring from his thigh at the base of a five-inch shard of metal still lodged in his leg.

"Don't move," Ava said, scrambling into her pack.

But Zach, of course, moved. And in the worst possible way too, realizing what was causing the blood... the pain. His hand flew to the shard and yanked, tearing the metal free from his leg.

The blood gushed faster.

Ava had never been one to get queasy at the sight of blood, but apparently when it's the man you've recently come to realize you loved, it wasn't so easy to keep your wits about you. Ava wanted to panic...had started to panic, but quickly realized she was all Zach had.

Come on, Ava, she said to herself. *Do not lose it. Keep your shit together and save the love of your life.*

An unexpected knock came at the front door.

The little girl's eyes grew wide...hopeful. Silly little bird, the Crow thought.

He picked the girl up off the sofa and carried her to a closet, tucking her gently inside.

He spoke quickly and quietly. "If you make a sound,

it will be very bad for both you and your daddy." He looked straight into her eyes as he finished speaking. "And believe me, you do not want that."

Needless to say, the hope vanished from the girl's eyes, replaced by a fear that sent a satisfied calm through him. He was in control of the situation. All was going as planned.

He just needed to take care of whatever this little problem was knocking on his door.

He wasn't worried. He was trained for this and would handle whatever stood in his way. He would not fail this time.

"Hello there," he said, a pleasant smile pasted on his face. The Crow was surprised, but not rattled, to see a uniformed officer standing at the door. "How can I help you?"

"Officer Banyan," the uniform said. "I'm checking on some leads in the area." He peered over the Crow's shoulder, looking for clues, perhaps anything suspicious. Looking for mistakes.

But the Crow did not make mistakes. "Oh?" he said. "What do you mean by leads?"

"Well, there have been a few odd occurrences back in Ambrosia Falls, and I ran into a fellow from—" he flipped back a few pages in his notebook "—Pieville, down there at the apple festival thing, and he remembered something strange. He said the property in the woods should be empty right now. Said the owners headed down to Florida for a couple of weeks. But then he saw smoke from an outdoor fire the other day, and thought it was strange. And since I was asking him about anything strange he might have noticed, he filled me in," the officer said. "Thought I ought to come out here and take a look."

Damn snoopy small towns, the Crow thought, but he pulled out his best acting chops and feigned relief to the point of almost chuckling. "Well, I suppose that makes sense. I'm Jonathan, the Millers' son. And you're right, my parents did head down to Orlando for a bit. They asked me to come house-sit, though I didn't think I could until the last minute. I suppose that's why no one in town knew about me coming to stay." He finished off with a shrug he hoped said the whole thing was no big deal.

The officer nodded, buying his story hook, line, and sinker. *Sucker.* The Crow found people were quite trusting if you were nice to them. Even trained professionals.

Of course, no one ever expected anything bad to happen in a place like Ambrosia Falls, which made the whole thing about ten times easier. If it hadn't been for the real prize—the Sparrow—he wouldn't even consider a job like this that was, frankly, a waste of his talents.

But this was the job he'd been thinking about for five years. On top of the years he'd put into the target before that. So much time invested. So much at stake.

The only one that really mattered.

"The Millners' son, you say?" the officer asked.

Typical. The man was testing him.

"Miller," the Crow replied, trying not to take offence at the juvenile treatment. Reminding himself the man was simply doing his job.

"Miller, right, right," Banyan said. "And you're the son?"

"Right. Jonathan, sir."

"And you're out here all by yourself?"

"Just me and my typewriter," he said. "Taking the opportunity to do a little work on the old memoirs."

The officer raised his eyebrows, then wrote the information in his notepad. It was unlikely he'd call around to check on the story of Jonathan Miller, but the Crow had done his research anyway. Art and Eliza Miller did indeed have a son named Jonathan, and the Millers only bought the place in Ambrosia Falls a few years ago. The folks in town likely wouldn't know what Jonathan looked like. Even if word got around the son was staying at the property, the Crow had no doubt he could deal with a few nosy neighbors. Maybe he'd tell them he was there for some peace and quiet and wasn't interested in getting to know the locals. The people in town wouldn't understand. Small-town people tended to live in small towns because they liked the socialization of knowing everyone around them, but they would let it go. They certainly wouldn't want to be accused of being something so heinous as "rude." They'd chalk it up to him being a "big city person," accompanying the phrase with knowing looks to their fellow gossips.

Even if a neighbor did show up, word would get around fast and that would be the end of it.

"So, uh, what did you mean about odd occurrences?" the Crow asked.

It was always better to keep a person talking, and not give them too much time to think. All the better for making people believe you're friendly and concerned, and if you were friendly and concerned, you were no longer a person worthy of suspicion.

Banyan waved a hand as if it were no big deal. "Some small petty crime stuff. Nothing major. Kids, I suspect."

The Crow made an agreeing, musing sound. "Probably bored in a place like this," he said, smiling at Banyan like he knew what he was talking about.

Banyan played right along as if the Crow had scripted the whole thing. "You got that right," he said with a chuckle. "Sorry to have bothered you. You have a good night now."

"Will do. Thanks, Officer," the Crow said, giving the man a wave as he turned to leave.

What a doofus, was all the Crow could think as the officer stepped off the porch and headed to his car.

Chapter 14

Officer Banyan got into his car, careful not to look back at the house too much.

He had good instincts, and those instincts were telling him the man in that house was not telling the whole truth. In fact, he'd be surprised if he'd been told even a sliver of truth.

It wasn't so much that the guy was suspicious, it was that he was too smooth about the whole interaction. People tended to be nervous around the law, like that guy back at the bakery, but this guy was a little too sure of himself.

Banyan turned around in the wide yard and made his way back down the drive. He was out of sight of the house in a few seconds, the forest swallowing his car. He drove another minute before he got to the side road he'd seen earlier, and turned onto it, pulling his car to the edge to make a call.

"Hey, Vince," Jennifer, the dispatcher, said from the other end of the line. "How's it up there in Appleville, or whatever it's called?"

"Hey, Jen. It's…interesting."

"I bet," she said. "What can I do for you?"

"I need a lead checked out if you have a minute. There's a couple out here—Art and Eliza Miller. I've got a guy here who says he's their son staying on the property. Can you find out if there's anything I need to know about this Jonathan Miller? Something's got my spidey senses twigging about him."

"Well, you do have the best spidey senses around," she said. "I'll see what I can find out."

"Thanks, Jen," Banyan said, and hung up.

Research always took its sweet time, and Banyan had never been very good at waiting. Besides, with all the convenient forest surrounding the house, it would be a real shame to let it go to waste. There weren't many surveillance opportunities better than the one presenting itself to him on a silver platter.

He quickly collected his supplies and headed into the trees.

The pain in Zach's leg made every minute feel more like an hour, and every step he took—leaning much more heavily on Ava than he would have liked—was like a fire poker being slowly inserted into his muscle, then down into the bone.

Ava had been incredible under pressure. The picture of calm in a world suddenly filled with pain and chaos and confusion and hurt. His thoughts circled around Chloe and what she must be going through, then to the pain in his leg that would not be ignored for more than a moment at a time, and then back to Chloe again.

The first-aid kit in his pack was almost used up, and they had to get to better supplies sooner rather than later.

"You're doing great," Ava said as she helped him hobble along through the rugged terrain.

She had to be as exhausted as he was, but she was much better at hiding it.

The trip back to the truck took far longer than the trip into the woods, and it was afternoon by the time they finally made it back.

"What are we going to do now?" Zach said, his voice choking.

Ava was helping him into the passenger side. "We're going to get you patched up, regroup, and decide what our next move is."

"We don't have time. We have to get to Chloe," he said, wincing as Ava started backing the truck out of the rugged terrain.

"I know," Ava said, "but we also have to stop the bleeding or you're going to pass out. And you're obviously no good to Chloe if you're unconscious."

No matter how much he wanted to argue, Zach knew she was right. He was weak and tired and needed to regain his strength.

It took several minutes to move through the not-quite-trail in reverse, but soon they were back on the road and rolling toward town. Somehow through the pain, Zach was able to find a few short bursts of something close to sleep—an intense sort of focused rest where he thought only of Chloe…of how they were going to get her back.

The trip felt long, but the clock confirmed they'd made good time. Ava must have driven way past the speed limit, and Zach was grateful for it.

Thankfully, their houses were at the end of their lane and backing the forest, so no one was around when they got back. Ava helped Zach out of the truck, his leg feeling like it had been lit on fire all over again.

"I have a good supply of first-aid stuff," Ava said, as she pointed him toward her house.

Zach didn't argue. Couldn't argue, really. Maybe it was the pain or maybe it was the stress, but he could hardly focus, let alone come up with a plan.

The bandage around his leg was soaked through as Ava helped lift him up each step, and slowly, painfully, they made their way into her house. Ava sat Zach down at the kitchen table.

"I'll be right back. Don't move," she said, as she went in search of supplies.

Moving was both the last thing Zach wanted to do, and the only thing he wanted to do. He had to get to Chloe. He leaned his head back, resting it against the wall behind him, no longer able to stop the tears from flowing. He wasn't sobbing, just a stream coming from the corners of his eyes as if he'd turned on a faucet.

"I'm so sorry, Zach," Ava whispered as she knelt beside him to deal with his leg. "I'm so sorry I've done this to you and Chloe."

Zach raised his head, about to speak, and realized Ava had her own tears teetering on the edge of her lower lids. But she was keeping herself busy, cutting off his pant leg and pulling the used bandage away from his wound, which was enough to shock him straight out of the conversation. He tensed and ground his jaws together, trying not to scream out with the pain.

But oddly, it seemed to shock his brain back into working again. "What about a drone?" he said, gritting his teeth.

"For?" Ava asked, unscrewing the cap from a bottle of something Zach was pretty sure was not going to feel all that wonderful.

"It can cover a hell of a lot more ground than we can," Zach said, just before he shouted a curse as the antiseptic hit his leg.

"That could work," Ava said, moving quickly to dry the gash as best as she could.

She grabbed a large wound closure bandage, adhering it to one side of the gash and then the other, then pulling the wound closed, the whole thing holding it shut like a series of connected butterfly bandages.

"This should hold for a while," Ava said, as she covered everything with a large gauze pad, then neatly wrapped it.

His leg still hurt like hell—was going to hurt like hell for a while, Zach knew—but it was clean and closed and, with any luck, would hold until he could get proper stitches. At least the damn air was off it anyway, and he could maybe have a chance at saving his daughter.

"Okay," Ava said, putting her hands up as if to surrender. "So, drone, then. You have one, right? You any good at flying it?"

Zach gave her a side-glance. "I'm okay," he said. "And I'm all we've got, so I'll have to make damned sure I'm at my best."

Ava nodded once. "Great, let's do it before we lose the light. Can you walk?"

Zach leaned heavily on the table as he made his way to his feet. He was going to walk one way or the other. "Yup, I'm good," he said, only wobbling a little when the head rush hit him.

He paused for a second, steadying himself, then headed toward the door. "I'm going to need help with the drone."

Ava followed, and ten minutes later they were loading the drone case into the truck. It was about the size of a carry-on suitcase but was reinforced with metal and was heavier than it looked.

"Let's go," Zach said, heading toward the driver's side.

"Not so fast," Ava said. "First off, you are not driving with that leg, and second, we need to gear up."

Gear up? Zach thought. Wondering if maybe she wanted to gather more food, some more water, which would probably be smart.

The pain in his leg had morphed into something more like a heavy, pulsing ache that was much better than the gaping wound had been. He limped up the porch stairs and stopped in the doorway as Ava pulled a large painting—apparently on hinges—from the wall and began punching numbers into a large safe behind it.

"Okay," he said, looking behind him, then quickly closing the door.

"There are some duffel bags in the chest behind you," she said, opening the door to the safe.

But Zach was too stunned, watching Ava pull weapons out of the safe, a handgun and several knives. She followed up with a magazine of ammo and what looked like a…grenade?

"What the hell?" Zach asked.

"I'll explain in the car," Ava said. "But we need those bags."

Zach nodded, then turned to the chest, lifting the lid to see four large duffels.

"We'll need them all," Ava said, heading to the kitchen table with her haul.

Zach looked at the duffels, then at the items Ava was carrying, then back at the duffels. There was no way what she was carrying would come close to filling one of the bags, let alone four, but he grabbed them anyway, his mind spinning.

Ava set everything on the table and moved to the stove, bending to open the warming drawer on the bottom. It didn't look like there was anything inside, but she reached under the lip of the drawer, struggling a bit with her burned arm, and released something with a soft click. The floor of the drawer lifted to reveal a false bottom from which Ava proceeded to pull four shotguns.

"Um, okay then," was about all Zach could say.

She didn't stop there. Moving to the living room, Ava lifted the seat of an easy chair to reveal yet another secret compartment, this one filled with what looked like high-tech equipment.

"Night vision with heat signature capabilities," she said, as casually as if she were reading the day's specials at Margie's Diner downtown.

Zach added the goggle-like contraptions to one of the bags.

Next, she moved the coffee table and pulled up the area rug, revealing a cutout in the floor. She pulled the switch completely off a nearby lamp and inserted it into a hole that looked like a knot in the wood. The switch became a handle, which Ava quickly pulled, revealing two more guns and some body armor.

Of course.

"Put this on," Ava instructed, tossing what Zach could only assume was a Kevlar vest his way.

Around the house they went, Ava revealing compartment after compartment filled with rations, weapons and ammo until each of the duffels was full and Zach was feeling a bit like he'd been launched off the planet and had landed in a different world.

Zach and Ava stood staring at the bags, so full it was a miracle the damn table was even holding.

He glanced at Ava, then looked at the bags, then looked at Ava again. "Who are you, and what have you done with my happy-go-lucky, always positive, charming and harmless best friend?"

Officer Banyan was perched in a prime spot inside the tree line overlooking the Miller property, which consisted of a few small outbuildings and a large barn, but he kept his eyes trained on the house. There hadn't been much movement, though he supposed there wouldn't be if the guy inside had been telling the truth and he was in there working on his memoirs.

He settled in to wait, binoculars in hand.

But it didn't take long to spot movement in the house.

The man, Jonathan, moved to one of the front windows and looked out. Then strangely, he moved on to another window on the side of the house that didn't even face the driveway and looked out that one too. He moved to the next window, went out of Banyan's sight for a few minutes—about the length of time he might need to look out a few more windows—then came back to the front of the house, looking in that direction one more time.

The man could have been admiring the scenery, Banyan supposed, but the way he was so methodical about it, almost tactical, something had to be up.

He lifted the binoculars and peered in, studying every detail in every corner of the house that was visible through the windows. He was about to pull back the binoculars and sit back for a bit when he spotted something rather disturbing.

A foot. And it most definitely did not belong to the man who answered the door. It was far too small, not to mention clad in a rainbow-striped sock. Banyan was the first to admit he didn't always catch every single detail, but he was sure he would have noticed bright, rainbow-striped socks if Jonathan—though he was beginning to doubt that was his real name—had been wearing them.

Unfortunately, the rest of the body the foot belonged to was out of sight.

He must have stared at the foot for ten minutes straight, until finally it twitched ever so slightly. Banyan let out a long breath, relieved the worst-case scenario, which had been strolling through his mind, was not reality.

Still, the man told him straight to his face he was there alone, and no matter which way you cracked that particular egg, the man had lied.

A few minutes later Banyan's phone vibrated.

"Hey, Vince," Jen said from the other end of the line.

"Hey, Jen," Banyan replied.

It was stunning how silent it was this far from civilization, and even though he was barely talking over a whisper, his voice cut through the quiet like a gunshot.

"I have your confirmation about that guy Jonathan,"

Jen said. "The Millers do, in fact, have a son by that name."

"So, he was telling the truth?" Banyan asked.

"Well, he didn't seem like a liar when I was talking to him."

"Wait, you talked directly to Jonathan Miller?"

"Just got off the phone with him," Jen confirmed.

Banyan's eyes shot back toward the forest house. "And did you happen to catch where he was at?"

"Sure did. Says he's packing for a trip to see his folks down in Florida. Leaves tomorrow," Jen said. "And Vince?"

"Yeah?"

"He says he's never been to his parents' place up in Ambrosia Falls. Been meaning to get there, but he usually just meets up with them in Florida once a year."

"I'll get back to you," Banyan said.

"Be careful out there, Vince," Jen said, hanging up.

Banyan's mind was whirling a mile a minute when he spotted movement in the house again. He quickly lifted his binoculars. The man—not Jonathan Miller, apparently—was bringing a plate of food over to the person who was just out of sight. The person did not reach for it, so the man eventually set the plate on the floor. Banyan peered through those binoculars so hard he forgot to blink, but the peering paid off. A few minutes later the person with the rainbow sock finally leaned forward to check out the plate of food.

Banyan wasn't sure what he'd expected, but an adorable preteen with an incredibly defiant look on her face had not been it.

Sure, a preteen could aim a defiant look at a parent,

but there was something in the way they interacted. This girl was not that man's kid.

It took Banyan about zero point five seconds to decide he had to get to her.

The correct thing to do would be to call for backup, but he decided he couldn't wait. He shot off a quick text, hoping it would reach its destination—cell service was spotty—then began the descent toward the house.

Still inside the protection of the trees, Banyan double-checked his equipment—handcuffs, gun loaded, holster unsnapped. He didn't like the feel of any of it. The remote location, the eerie silence, the child in harm's way. It was a cop's nightmare scenario, the kind that tested the mettle and let you know if you had what it took. And Banyan knew there was no way in hell he was turning around and leaving that little girl behind.

He considered how to approach the situation. He could simply walk up and knock on the door…a better option if he had his squad car with him. But out here on foot, he still had the element of surprise working for him.

Best case scenario would be if he could get the girl and haul ass out of there before the man even knew she was gone. But hiking a scared kid through dense forest after she'd been abducted and through who knew what was probably not the best situation either.

Banyan took a deep breath. There was a very good chance he was going to have to take a shot at the guy. With any luck, he wouldn't have to take a fatal shot, but he needed to prepare himself in case it came to that.

Banyan pulled the gun from his holster and stepped out into the clearing. He moved quickly and quietly toward the structure, flattening himself against the house near one of the side windows, hoping he'd catch a glimpse of the girl. He needed to know exactly where she was before anything happened. He couldn't risk hurting her and didn't want to traumatize her more by witnessing a shooting if it could be helped.

He tried to figure how an abduction of a girl could relate to the other incidents in town but couldn't understand what the connection might be. What he did know was, it was too small a town and too small a time frame for all of it to be coincidence. Something worse than anything the residents of a town like Ambrosia Falls had likely seen was happening, and the man inside was the key to unlocking it all. If Banyan could, he'd like to take the man alive, but the girl was the priority…if she was in danger, he would do what he had to do to ensure her safety.

There was no movement visible inside. Banyan made his way toward the front door, ducking under windows, then climbed the steps silently. He reached for the knob, which turned easily in his hand. He supposed the man inside wasn't too worried about security way out there in the middle of nowhere.

Banyan eased himself inside, gun at the ready, heart beating a million miles a minute. It took a few moments for his eyes to adjust to the dim entrance, but soon he was moving into the living room where he'd first seen the girl.

She was no longer there.

He moved stealthily across one wall of the living room, making his way toward the kitchen area, gun leading as he rounded the corner. Quickly and methodically, he cleared the room, moving deeper into the house, entering a hallway.

He was about to pass the first bedroom on the right, peeking in and seeing it was empty, when something caught his eye. Something flickering inside a smaller space—a closet—on the other side of the room. He moved toward the lights, realizing the flickering was a security setup. He moved closer, entering the walk-in closet. If he could get a good look at the monitors, maybe he could find the girl.

Three screens sat on a small desk. The first showed four views of the inside of the house—the living room, the kitchen and a couple bedrooms. The second monitor showed various sections of land surrounding the property. This was when Banyan's tap-dancing nerves began to whirl their way into a frenzy. The third screen showed flashing words. *Perimeter Breach, Northeast Quadrant.*

That was the moment he knew. The moment he realized he had lost the very second he stepped out of the trees.

He turned to leave the closet. To give himself a chance to get out of there alive, but the small space was already going dark. The door was shut, then bolted behind him even though closet doors didn't typically have bolts on them.

The man had prepared the closet for this exact purpose. To lure anyone wanting to help straight there. And as a fog-like substance began filling the small space, the feeds on the first monitor changed, the girl popping up clearly on the screen. She was in a dark space, alone and looking pissed off...and scared. Banyan called out to her, yelled that he was there to help.

But he couldn't help. And the girl showed no signs of having heard him before his head became heavy and he slid down the wall.

His last thought before everything went black was, *I failed her.*

Chapter 15

Ava and Zach were heading back to the forest. Unfortunately, they didn't have a specific target this time.

What they did have was about half an hour before they reached the last clear area appropriate for launching a drone before the forest got heavier.

Zach finally broke the silence. "So, I'm guessing there's a little more to your past than you've led me to believe."

Ava let out a long, slow sigh. This was the moment she'd been dreading for five years. The moment the people important to her found out she wasn't exactly who she said she was. She wasn't anything even close to the person she appeared to be.

"I'm so sorry, Zach. It was all part of the conditions of being in witness protection. Though it's not strictly witness protection in my case, more like asset protection."

"So you're an asset of the government."

"I used to be," Ava said. "But I haven't been active since I came to Ambrosia Falls. Everything about my life here has been legit since the day I arrived."

She hoped he understood that meant her feelings for him too—especially her feelings for him.

"So…judging from the arsenal you've got back there, were you some kind of assassin or something?"

Now that she had come this far, she couldn't lie to him anymore. Found she didn't want to keep anything from him anymore.

"Sometimes," Ava said, watching him out of the corner of her eye, but his face remained neutral. "And sometimes I was recon, and sometimes I was asked to be security, or backup, or sometimes I was needed for my expertise."

"Expertise in what? Were there a lot of national baking emergencies?" Zach asked, though his voice sounded more baffled than angry. More stunned than sarcastic.

"Baking has always just been a hobby," Ava said.

"Could've fooled me," Zach replied, and Ava smiled.

"I have an advanced degree in geology. I specialize in forensic geology, using trace evidence to track down suspects or persons of interest. I often got asked to assist in time-sensitive searches for victims or sometimes perpetrators. I have some sharpshooting too, so that was a big part of my job."

Zach swallowed hard.

"I'm still me though," she said.

"Still you. Right. You just have a little forensic geologist slash sharpshooter experience to pad your résumé with. No big deal, right?"

"I'm serious, Zach. This doesn't change who I've always been to you."

Zach shook his head, still clearly trying to wrap it around everything.

"And now that you know," Ava continued. "it means I don't have to hide any of this—" she waved her hand toward the bags in the back seat "—and we can go in there and get Chloe back using everything we've got available to us."

"That's the other thing I've been wondering about," Zach said. "Why the hell didn't you tell me all this when Chloe got taken? Why did we go up to that shack and make damn fools of ourselves falling right into his trap?"

"That's on me," Ava said. "I didn't think Justin would be so organized, so prepared. None of that was ever his strong suit. It's why he and I worked so many jobs together. I was the one who checked and rechecked each tiny detail of every job. He was the one who was good at storming in and causing chaos, which is a surprisingly rare quality to have, and if there was ever a master at it, it was Justin. This whole…careful, methodical, calculated side is something I've never seen from him before."

"So you underestimated him," Zach said, his voice accusatory.

"I'm not so sure it was underestimation so much as it was familiarity and knowledge of past behavior and skills. You want to know a target inside and out, which is why I thought I had an advantage here, but clearly Justin has changed as much as I have. Maybe more."

"Well, you did get one thing right, at least," Zach said. "This is all on you. And I may never see my daughter again. Sometimes, I wish I'd never met you."

The words stung. More than stung, they obliterated. And the worst part was, he was absolutely right.

Zach hated himself the moment the words left his mouth. He was hurt and angry and maybe a little embarrassed it had taken so long to catch on to the truth of who Ava really was. And worse, he was running on fear, terrified something unthinkable could have already happened to Chloe.

They drove in silence for a while, but when they neared their destination, Zach couldn't take it anymore. "I'm sorry," was all he said.

Ava shrugged one shoulder. "You're not wrong. I did do this. I came into this town and into your lives out of nowhere. You didn't ask for any of it. I knew the risks, and I decided to get close to you and Chloe anyway. And as long as I live, it will be the biggest regret of my life."

Oof. Zach knew Ava was talking about putting them in harm's way, but it still stung to hear the woman he loved say she regretted ever knowing him. Of course, he had just told her the same thing only more harshly, so yeah. He could only hope she meant the words about as much as he did, which was not at all.

"And don't worry," she continued. "As soon as we get Chloe back, you'll never have to see me again—but I am trained for this sort of thing and probably your best chance at getting her back."

"Ava, that's not what—"

Ava put up a hand. "It's fine. It's…whatever. Right now, we need to focus on Chloe. She's all that matters."

Zach certainly couldn't argue with that, and they were nearing the edge of the trees anyway, so he let it drop. Ava pulled the truck into an approach off the road, stopping before they went too far down the rugged trail leading into a wheat field.

Ava opened the tailgate and pulled the drone case to the edge. Zach took over from there, opening the case and pulling the drone from the protective foam padding. He was about to walk it a few paces away, but Ava took it gently from his hands. Walking was not his strong suit at the moment.

Zach powered everything up, and within a few minutes, the drone was airborne, hovering high over the trees.

"This could take a while," Zach said. "There's a lot of area to cover in these trees."

Ava nodded. "It's what makes it perfect for hiding." She shook her head. "I should have anticipated this. The people who put me here should have anticipated this."

"I'm not sure there's a place in the world that doesn't have trees close by."

"Not this kind of dense forest though. A person could get lost in this indefinitely."

Zach focused on flying the drone and trying not to get discouraged. Not yet.

Ava shook out her body. "Okay, this isn't helping. I need to think. Think like Justin, only not exactly like Justin since he's been ahead of us this whole time."

"Okay, so what's his usual MO?"

"He's never been good at being uncomfortable," Ava said. "Or at being wrong. Which is probably why he's still after me after all these years."

"Why was he after you in the first place?" Zach asked.

It was the question he'd been wondering since he found out someone had been after her. He'd assumed she'd gotten swept up in the wrong crowd and witnessed something she shouldn't have, but that theory didn't really fly anymore.

"I can only assume he was an enemy operative. A sort of double agent, I guess, although we don't use that term in the real world. It's more of a TV thing."

Zach nodded, thinking over all the things that meant. "And you were with him for a while?"

"Years," Ava said, rubbing the bridge of her nose, like she was trying to stop a tingle. "I found his stash of surveillance on me. All the years we'd been together, and for a while before that even. He'd been gathering data, intel for who knows what purpose. He had a thousand opportunities to kill me... I don't know why he never did. I almost wish he would have," she said, trailing off.

There was a pause as Zach looked at her—beautiful, vulnerable, still the Ava he knew, just...with a few additional skills.

"I'm glad he didn't," Zach said.

Maybe it was the hope talking, but he couldn't bring himself to believe he would never see Chloe again. And knowing what he knew about Ava now actually made him feel better about the situation. Yes, he was still terrified beyond belief, but in a way, none of it seemed real. He still felt Chloe's presence, and he was going to cling to that feeling as hard as he damn well could.

Ava began to pace, thinking, mumbling a bit to herself, though Zach couldn't catch any of the words. He was busy trying not to let his drone crash. It had been a while since he'd been out flying, and the machine took more concentration than one might think.

"You wanna talk it out?" he asked.

Ava stopped and turned to him. "Maybe."

"Okay, so it was a surprise to you that he headed for the shack, I'm guessing."

"Very much so," Ava said, "but I figured he was trying to throw me off his trail. And I hate that it worked."

"It's smart, but we can be smarter. So, he had it pretty cushy at the first place he was at...the Lawson place."

Ava nodded. "It made sense because it was close. It

was cushy enough for him…barely," she said, rolling her eyes, "and the family was going to be away for a while."

"But he likely guessed you'd know all that about him, so he set it up so you would think you were getting the jump on him, when really, he was ten steps ahead."

"I hope not ten," Ava said, "but yeah, sounds about right."

"And then the shack."

"Which we can assume he only went to long enough to plant the explosives and take the photo of Chloe," Ava said.

"Right. And had we been thinking in terms of Justin, we might have realized it was a trap, but we were so focused on Chloe. I'd bet my last dollar he purposely got the window in the picture so he could throw us off the scent of where he was really staying."

"So where would he really be staying then?" Ava asked, more to herself than to Zach.

She started pacing again.

"Well, we know he likes a luxurious place if he can get it," Zach said, the wheels starting to turn a little faster up in the old hamster wheel of his.

"But we thought he'd stay close to town, which is why I headed to the subdivision on the lake first," Ava continued.

"But then he headed for the woods, which was smart. Easy to get lost. But if this was the place he'd planned on staying for the major part of his, what would you call it?" Zach asked.

"Operation," Ava said.

"Right. For the major part of this operation, I'd bet he'd still be looking for a nice, cushy place."

"If that even existed," Ava said, still pacing.

"Ah, but it does," Zach said, his heart rate climbing with a little zip of excitement. "The Miller place," he said, with a big smile.

"Who are the Millers?" Ava asked. "I thought I knew everyone in Ambrosia Falls."

"You do, but the Millers get their mail in Pieville."

Ava's eyes grew wide. "Can you find their place with the drone?"

"I think so," Zach said, quickly changing course.

Several minutes later Zach was maneuvering the drone over a patch of forest about twelve miles away. "I don't know exactly where it is, I've never been out there, but Arnie Jackson was out helping build it about ten years ago. Said the place was huge. They built it on an old ranch site, apparently."

"Sounds like it would be the perfect place for Justin," Ava said, looking like she didn't particularly like the taste of his name on her tongue.

"But wouldn't he realize we'd figure it out eventually?" Zach asked, his eyes glued to the monitor, praying for a break in the trees.

"That's exactly what he's counting on," Ava said. "He wants me to come to him."

Zach swallowed. He very much did not like the sound of that.

Just then, off to the far side of the monitor, Zach spotted something. The edge of a clearing. He quickly maneuvered the drone toward the clearing, hoping the machine was too high for the whir to be heard from the ground.

"I've got something," Zach said.

Ava came to stand beside him, leaning toward the small screen.

"That's got to be it," she said.

"Has to be. There's a vehicle in the drive."

"Could be the Millers'," Ava said.

"Could be," Zach agreed. "I wish I knew more about them."

"Wait, what's that?" Ava asked, pointing to something shiny in the trees.

Zach changed the path of the drone again, centering over the object in question. "Is that a car?"

"I think so," Ava said. "Weird place for a car. And what's that dark strip on the top?"

"Holy shit. I think it's a police vehicle," Zach said, panic sneaking into his voice. "The asshole said no cops. Why the hell are there cops?" He turned to Ava, his eyes wide. "Maybe they have Chloe already. We have to get out there."

Ava remained silent.

Chapter 16

At least we have a new target, Ava thought as she steered the truck toward their destination. But she was worried. The police car presented a whole host of new problems, and she did not like adding variables to the mix. And a cop was a huge variable.

Sure, there was a chance the officer had somehow caught on to Justin, taken him down and rescued Chloe, but that was very unlikely. Still, the police vehicle was well hidden from both the road and the place where Justin was squatting, so maybe he or she was just watching. Waiting for backup. Of course, that meant another set of eyes on their rescue, which could go either way. A cop could think they were the bad guys and keep them from doing what they needed to do. Or they could decide to help.

The fact that Justin specifically said no cops did not put her at ease. He would have to know she had nothing to do with this officer showing up—they'd been trained to work outside the confines of organized law enforcement, at least the kind the public knew about, anyway. The "no cops" thing had been for Zach's sake. People who'd lived their whole lives following the law would automatically think to phone the police, but Ava was far beyond any of that. If there was anything she couldn't take care of herself, she had resources beyond typical law enforcement.

Maybe the whole police vehicle thing was another ploy by Justin to throw her off her game. She just couldn't figure out what the reasoning behind it might be.

It took time to get out to the remote location. More time than it did getting to the place they could park before they went on foot to the shacks, but this time they wouldn't have to trek so far through the forest.

"I think we should stay away from the police car," Ava said. "On the off chance it's a plant by Justin to mess with us, we won't want to get too close."

"A plant?"

Ava shrugged. "I can't figure out any good reason to do something like that, but if there's one thing I've learned over the past few days, it's that I do not have as much insight into Justin's thinking as I thought I did. It could simply be something he's using to distract us, so we'll miss something else. We need to stay alert…be ready for anything."

"I don't know how to be ready for anything," Zach said.

"Just try not to be too surprised, no matter what happens."

Zach raised an eyebrow. "Considering our current situation, and the things I've discovered about the person I'm closest to, I'd say you could pretty much send a steamroller right over me and I'd say it was par for the course."

"Good," Ava said, trying to ignore the sarcasm laced in his words.

It would be good if he was angry. Even better that he

was angry with her. It would mean Chloe was his only priority. Maybe, with any luck, he wouldn't worry too much about what she was doing.

Because she was going after Justin. And she wouldn't let a little thing like her personal safety get in the way. She would end this one way or the other. If Justin was gone, there'd be no more threat to Chloe and Zach. And the same applied if she was the one who was gone instead. Either way, she was going to make sure Chloe and Zach were safe.

"We're getting close," Zach said, watching the pin he'd dropped on his phone map based on the drone footage. He hoped he wouldn't lose the signal, since cell service was pretty spotty in the area.

"The police car is in there, I think," Ava said, pointing to the recently car-trampled grass leading into the ditch.

A short distance later they approached the gravel drive leading into the acreage and up to the farmyard. From the drone, it had looked like the house was about a half mile in. The place must be a nightmare in the winter. A person could be stranded there for days if they didn't have a snowplow of some sort.

"I'm going to go past. See if there's somewhere we can ease into the trees like the police car did."

Zach nodded, his neck craning to see as far as he could up the drive, which, given the sharp curve near the entrance, was not far at all.

About a quarter mile past the turnoff, Ava eased the truck off the road and into the ditch, continuing through a small break in the trees. She weaved a little way farther until she was sure the vehicle couldn't be seen from the road. The grass would be trampled, just like with the police car, but there wasn't much she could do about that.

"We need to go up the hill and try to get a read on the place," Ava said. "Figure out what our next move is going to be."

"I don't like this," Zach said. "Chloe is in there all alone. He's one guy. With all this firepower, we should be charging in there and taking him down."

Ava shook her head. "That's way too risky for Chloe. What if she got caught in the line of fire? Justin may know he needs Chloe for leverage to get me out here, but once I'm in his line of sight, he won't think twice about using her for a shield."

Zach cursed under his breath. "I hate this."

"I hate it too," Ava said. "We can't carry all this up the hill. Take what you're comfortable with and follow me," she told him, tucking a handgun into the back of her pants and a knife at her ankle. She hung the infrared goggles around her neck.

"We'll come back for what we need once we know what we're up against."

Zach rummaged through the bags while Ava doublechecked her ammo. "Do you need help with any of that?"

"I think I'm okay. I haven't used one of these in years," he said, checking a gun of his own, "but I do know a bit. Like I said, I used to hunt."

Ava nodded once. "Sounds good," she said, hoping Zach would not have to use his weapon. If the guy was against hunting animals, who knew what it might do to him to aim at a person.

They moved up the hill quickly, slowing as they neared the top. Staying low, Zach followed Ava as she crept to the point where she could see the farmyard. All was still and quiet.

Ava put the goggles on, then began to whisper as Zach crept up beside her. She lowered to her stomach and Zach followed suit.

"So, these don't work like they do in the movies," Ava said. "We're not going to be able to see the outline of a person unless they're outside. Through walls we have to use our best guesses. Walls are insulated and aren't the best way to get a good read, but we might get lucky and catch someone walking past a window or something."

Zach was disappointed, but realized there wasn't much he could do about it. He nodded and put his goggles on anyway.

"I can't stand sitting here waiting for something to happen," Zach said. "I need to get to Chloe. She must be so scared."

"I know," Ava whispered, "but this is the way it has to be. If we go in there unprepared, the person we're putting most at risk is Chloe, and that is the last thing we want to do."

"I get that in my head, but this is killing me. I need to know if she's down there."

"Give it a few minutes," Ava said, studying every inch of the yard, searching for anything out of the ordinary. "Looks like there's a heat spot inside the barn."

"Just one?" Zach asked, turning his attention to the barn.

"I think so. Like I said, it's hard to tell through walls."

"So, let's go in there and get him," Zach said.

"Except we don't know it's him. It could be Chloe, or even an animal."

"If it's Chloe, that's even better, we can grab her and get the hell out of here."

"Assuming it's not a trap," Ava said.

Zach let out a long sigh. He just wanted to know his kid was okay and get her to safety.

"Look, I know this is hard. It's killing me too," Ava said. "But we have to play this smart. If it's Chloe, great, but there's no telling what kind of trap he may have set. And if it's Justin in there, things could get ugly fast, and if he goes down—" she let out a long sigh "—we need to know where she is before anything can happen to Justin."

Zach understood what Ava was getting at then. "In case he has her stashed somewhere it'll be hard to find her."

Ava nodded, not looking at all happy he'd arrived on the same page.

They lay in silence for a few minutes, watching… waiting. Zach's thoughts jumped from being certain something catastrophic could have happened to being so sure Chloe was alright. Because she had to be. Any other outcome was unthinkable. Any future without her was impossible. And then his thoughts moved to scolding. Cursing himself for even thinking about any of that when all his attention should be 100 percent on getting to her. Rescuing her. Making sure she was okay and spoiling her for the rest of her life. And yeah, in his head he knew spoiling her wasn't good for her in the long run, but that didn't stop him from making pleas with the universe that if she ended up okay, he would do anything and everything in his power to make this up to her.

But being stuck inside his own head was not helping anyone, least of all Chloe.

"What are you thinking?" Zach asked.

"It's so quiet. Too quiet," Ava said. "Too still."

"Do you think he's not even here?" Zach asked, his disappointment already rising.

"No, I think he's here somewhere," Ava said. "It's like I can feel him, but something isn't right. If he had a plan, there would be something obvious, or at least a hint at something. I can't figure out what his strategy is."

"I bet that's exactly what he's hoping for," he said. "Get you off your game. Get you lost inside your head, guessing what his next move is going to be."

Ava nodded. "Yeah, and I've been thinking about that. Trying to decide whether he'd do something exactly opposite of what I would expect, or if that's too predictable now too."

"If it were me, I'd do both," Zach said.

"Me too," Ava agreed. "Which means we have nothing. No strategy."

"We have instinct," Zach said, "and mine is telling me to get back to the vehicle, load up with as much shit as we can possibly carry, get Chloe out of there and end this bastard."

Ava nodded. "I guess waiting isn't getting us anywhere at this point. You sure you're up for this? Going up against Justin is no joke."

"I couldn't give a flying rat's butt who we're going up against. It's not about him."

"I'm not sure there are flying rats—at least I hope to hell there aren't—but I get what you're saying," Ava said, easing her way down the low hill a bit, then slowly standing.

Zach followed, but he had only taken a few steps before the ground beneath them shook. The world in front of them lit up in a series of flashes, one after the other. The noise was booming, shattering the serenity of the forest.

"Holy shit," Zach said.

Ava stood motionless, mouth hanging open.

"Ava?" Zach asked. He'd never seen her in shock like this, and if she—the trained spy-type professional person, or whatever, exactly, she was—was in shock, things must be very bad indeed.

"I think we can assume Justin knows we're here," Ava said, her eyes still wide with a sort of faraway look in them. "I'm pretty sure that was your truck."

"Along with all of our ammo and guns?" Zach asked, his voice squeaking a little.

Ava nodded.

"We have to get to Chloe now!" Zach said. "Please tell me we can go find her now. We have to get her away from this guy."

Ava looked from Zach to the area where the truck had exploded, then back to Zach again, her face finally morphing from shock to something closer to determination. "Yeah, we gotta go now," she said, turning toward the house.

Zach was on her heels. "What's the plan?"

"I have absolutely no idea."

Chapter 17

Since Justin clearly had the advantage of location and planning, Ava had hoped to even the playing field with the element of surprise and sheer firepower, both of which had just blown up right in front of her face.

He'd known exactly what her plan had been. It was a thought that sent stone-cold fear through every inch of her body. She always thought she'd be able to outsmart Justin when the time came, but she realized he'd had five years to plan what to do when he found her. Five years she'd spent rebuilding her life instead of thinking about Justin.

They'd been the best five years of her life, and she wanted to end this asshole for making her go back to her old life. How could she have fallen for his BS in the first place? She'd always been the better operative—more careful, more intuitive, more prepared. But now she wondered if all that had been true, or if he'd played it that way all along and she was simply the world's biggest sucker.

The worst part was that now—when her skills and confidence mattered the most—was not the time to start doubting her abilities, to start feeling inadequate.

She had to save a beautiful, smart, hilarious little girl,

and save her dad while she was at it. If she could just do that, she'd gladly lay down her life and give Justin what he wanted. What happened to her after Zach and Chloe were safe mattered exactly zero percent.

"Are we going for the barn?" Zach asked.

"Probably," Ava said, slowing down as they neared the edge of the trees.

She motioned for Zach to stop, as she eased behind a large tree. Zach did the same a few feet away.

"I want to check the heat signature one more time," she said. "Might look different now that we're closer."

She pulled the googles up from around her neck. Zach did the same with his.

"Shit," Ava said, closing her eyes to the blinding light.

Zach made a surprised sound as the same glare burned into his eyes. "Jesus, what the hell is that?"

"He must have lit a bunch of fires in there," Ava said, trying to blink the bright spots from her vision.

"How is it not burning down then?"

"Not sure," Ava said. "They must be contained somehow. Maybe in metal containers or something."

"I am really starting to hate this guy," Zach said, throwing out the greatest understatement Ava had ever heard.

"Yeah, welcome to the club," she said, with a half-hearted smirk.

"He clearly wants us to go into that barn," Zach said. "Which means I am highly disinclined to do so."

Ava thought for a moment. Zach was right. Justin obviously wanted them in the barn...using the fires as a sort of calling card slash bait situation. So that was exactly where Ava was going to go. But she sure as hell wasn't letting Zach get anywhere near it.

"Let's go for the house," Ava said. "Stay low. You go around the front, and I'll take the back. With any luck we can catch him by surprise from one angle or the other."

She pulled the gun from her waistband and nodded for Zach to do the same.

"Promise me one thing," she said. "If you find Chloe first, get her out. Don't worry about where I am. Your only job is to get her out—I'll be right behind you."

The moment Zach gave his nod, Ava sprinted from the trees and headed toward the back of the house, clearing the corner of it in seconds. A quick glance back assured her Zach was headed toward the front of the house. She waited a few more beats, hoping to hell it would either take Zach a bit to get inside, or there wouldn't be a good view toward the barn from in there. She didn't need a lot of time, but if he spotted her, everything would be lost. There was a still a chance she could handle Justin if left to her own devices, but she definitely wouldn't be able to handle him if she had to make sure Zach was safe too.

If she knew Justin at all—though after the past couple of hours, she wasn't sure she ever did—he would be focused on one thing and one thing only.

Her.

And maybe it was instinct, or maybe it was the fact that she felt like she did still know the Crow, at least in the most fundamental sense, but Ava somehow knew Chloe was not in that barn. He would be keeping her somewhere that wouldn't be easy to find. He wanted to keep Zach busy…keep him away.

And to have her, his Sparrow, all to himself for one last fight.

* * *

Zach tried like hell to get his hands to stop shaking but was having no luck. It had to be the nerves or adrenaline or something, but either way, he took a moment—just a second—to breathe and try to center himself. The life of his daughter depended on what he did in the next few minutes.

Thank the Lord Ava was right there with him. He wasn't alone. Chloe wasn't alone.

Two breaths in, two breaths out, then he tried the door.

Locked.

He wondered if the real owners of the house ever locked their doors. They were so deep into the middle of nowhere it seemed impossible some random criminal would stumble upon the place, but he supposed no one was ever completely immune to the outside world encroaching into their existence. The current situation was proof enough of that.

There was little reason to worry about noise—Justin clearly knew they were there—but Zach's instincts told him to be as quiet as possible. Still, the only way in seemed to be to break one of the small windowpanes on the door and reach in to unlock the door like they always did on TV. He was about to do it too, when he noticed an open window halfway down the side of the house. He figured it would be a whole lot quieter to cut through a window screen than it would be to smash a damn pane of glass.

He just needed to find something to step onto to get up to the window. Anything would do, like…one of the chairs sitting around the firepit a few yards away. He rushed over and grabbed one, hoping Ava wasn't already inside and wondering where in the hell he was.

He made quick work of the screen with his pocketknife and eased one leg over the windowsill, pushing off with his other leg to sort of jump up there. And damn if it didn't hurt quite a bit more than he expected with the gaping wound that had only been closed a short while earlier.

He bit his lip through the pain as he struggled through the window.

It was not a graceful endeavor.

He glanced around, taking in the room, half expecting Ava to already be far enough into the house to catch a glimpse of her, but she was nowhere to be found. Maybe she was halfway to clearing the whole place by now, Zach thought, and figured he'd better get a move on if he was to be of any use at all.

He began on the main floor, moving through the living room, eyes darting, ears perked, skin prickling with adrenaline and anticipation. Easing his way toward what he thought might be the kitchen, he peeked around the corner. It was, in fact, a kitchen, and it was very empty and very quiet.

Zach let out a long, slow breath, trying to find his composure, his bravery, his wits. And while he was pretty sure he didn't actually find any of those things, desperation and fear propelled him forward anyway.

Where the hell was Ava? He did not think he would be doing this alone.

But he was so close to Chloe now. He could feel it.

Moving back through the living room, he started down a short hallway. Peeking into the first room on the right, he found a bedroom. Nothing seemed out of the ordinary. Without going in, he moved on to the next bedroom down the hall. Same thing. The third bedroom was as empty as the others. His frustration grew as he moved to the bathroom at the end of the hall, even flinging the shower curtain open and half-expecting someone to jump out at him.

He had "cleared" all the rooms and come up with nothing. But of course, he hadn't really cleared them completely, had he? He'd determined there was no one obvious lurking in any of them, but he had to look closer. Closest to the third bedroom, he moved into that room first, gun at the ready. He whipped the door back and pointed his gun in that direction, heart beating hard and feeling like an absolute imposter. Who was he trying to kid? He had no idea what he was doing. Still, what other choice did he have?

Zach ducked and lifted the bedspread, readying for the jump scare of his life, but again, nothing happened. He moved on to the closet, taking a deep breath before thrusting the door open then aiming the gun into every corner.

Empty.

He really hoped no one was watching him, because this whole daring rescue thing was making him feel like the biggest amateur on the planet.

He moved into the next bedroom across the hall, going through all the same motions with the same result.

Zach headed down the hall, backtracking his way to the first bedroom. He did the behind the door thing, the under the bed thing, then moved on to the closet. But this time, when he moved to the closet, he wasn't met with nothing.

There was a latch on the door.

On the outside. His heart began to race. There would never be a latch on the outside of a closet door unless someone on the outside was keeping someone on the inside against their will.

Zach slowly opened the latch, visions of Chloe jumping into his arms already rolling through his mind as he whipped the door open.

The first thing he registered was that Chloe was not there. His heart fell straight to his feet and through the floor.

The second thing he registered was even though Chloe wasn't there, the closet was not empty. A man lay on the floor, and Zach couldn't tell whether he was dead or passed out. A strange shot of excitement moved through him…if this was Justin, then maybe everything was already okay. Maybe Ava had somehow gotten in there and secured him in the small space, perhaps already on her way to Chloe. Unfortunately, the third thing he registered was that the man was wearing a police uniform, and also, that he looked familiar.

Shit.

The cop from that morning in town. Banyan?

He had no idea how the officer had gotten to Justin ahead of them, but it actually made Zach feel more secure, his shoulders easing a bit. The police knew what they were doing. Except, he realized in the next heartbeat, even if Banyan had found Justin, he hadn't fared too well going up against him, and the low vibration of dread in his stomach started all over again.

Guess they knew the origin of the police cruiser in the woods now.

And then, as these things rushed through his mind, Zach registered a fourth thing. There was a strange smell in the room…a little bit earthy, and a lot chemical. He looked at the officer on the floor. Had the man been gassed?

Without thinking, Zach just moved. And yeah, probably not the best idea to go rushing into a small space that might still be filled with gas, but that apparently didn't matter to his brain. He shoved the gun into the back of his pants, then grabbed the man under the armpits, gathering all his strength to pull him out of there.

The thought had occurred to him that maybe it was already too late, and perhaps he shouldn't be moving a body—especially if this place was about to become a crime scene—but even as he was thinking those things, Zach knew he couldn't leave a defenseless man in a situation like that, even if it might already be too late.

After a few strong heaves, Zach maneuvered the officer out of the closet and into the bedroom. He thought about putting him on the bed, but all of a sudden, he was feeling a little…dizzy?

His breathing was heavy from the excursion. Which meant he'd taken in some of the gas. He hoped to hell it wasn't lethal, and hoped to even deeper depths of hell this asshole hadn't done anything like this to Chloe.

Zach had never been so scared, so full of adrenaline, so motivated to…he wasn't sure what. Find Chloe, for sure, but then he wanted to do something else. To find this man who had his daughter and make sure he never did anything like this to anyone ever again.

He did not like the feeling. It wasn't him.

The air in the bedroom was probably already compromised, but in Zach's mind, it only made sense to shut the closet door and keep as much of it contained to that small space as possible. But when he moved toward the closet, he saw the screens. Four of them, clearly receiving pictures from surveillance cameras around the property.

He was torn. This could be the answer to exactly where Chloe was, not to mention where Ava had gotten to, but getting close enough to see, and maybe even figure out the basics of the system, would mean going all the way inside the closet and risking getting caught in there himself...maybe permanently.

The room seemed to tilt around him.

But the other choice was to continue wandering around the house aimlessly, and then move on to the grounds if he had no luck. But all of this was already taking too long. Every second Chloe was out there, scared and alone, was one second too many.

He almost decided it wasn't worth the risk. He was of no use to Chloe or anyone else if he was unconscious... or worse, and he moved to close the door, ready to seal it shut and latch it back up, but then a flash. Movement across one of the screens and he was pulled in, as if he had no control over his feet. He yanked his shirt up over his nose, realizing it wasn't going to help much, but it was all the protection he had and peered into the screen.

But the screen was so dark, like maybe he hadn't actually seen anything at all.

He blinked, then blinked again, convincing himself it had been a trick of the eye. He'd wanted so badly to see something that he dreamed it all up.

He started backing out of the closet when the flash came again. Someone running across the top left screen. The feed was dim, but the place looked like…the barn. And someone had just moved from behind one large beam to the next.

Ava.

What the shit was Ava doing in the barn?

But Zach knew the answer with a certainty that sent a chill straight to his bones. She was going after Justin, and she was doing it alone. Except screw that, Zach thought, already halfway there in his mind. He didn't think about what he would do when he got there; he only knew he had to help.

And then the screens all flashed, changing to new feeds, and he saw the one thing he'd been hoping to see, so scared he might never see again.

The face of his beautiful daughter.

Chapter 18

The barn door slid open with a wail. So much for taking the sneaky route, Ava thought as she eased inside. Even though the sun was just beginning to set, the inside of the barn was incredibly dim, and her eyes needed time to adjust. Time she didn't have.

Ava's first instinct was to slide the door shut again, though it did cross her mind she might need a quick escape. But the thought of Justin being able to get out without her realizing it and going after Zach or Chloe won out, and she squeak-slid the door shut again.

Her eyes still a bit compromised, Ava felt like a fish in a fishbowl—vulnerable...exposed. She needed to find cover.

She began to make out shapes in the shadows. The place was a veritable smorgasbord of farm implements ranging from large tractors and machinery all the way down to pitchforks and rakes, and a million other potentially deadly instruments in between.

The infrared goggles were useless. Justin had set at least a dozen fires in the main open space of the barn, contained in old wheel wells on top of concrete blocks. It was a maze in there, with stalls running in one direction, then turning and continuing in another. Which would have been fine if Justin hadn't already had time to memorize the place.

First rule of operatives—know the territory. Which went hand in hand with the second rule—confuse your opponent whenever possible.

It was a built-in element of surprise situation on repeat.

"Hello, Sparrow," a creepily disembodied voice echoed through the barn.

What the hell had he done? Install a damned speaker system?

"I've been waiting for this moment for a long time."

It's funny the things a person forgot when given ample amounts of time. Ava was surprised to learn she'd forgotten his voice. Or not forgotten it, really, but it had been such a long time since she'd thought about his voice, the sound of it took her by surprise. Made so many memories come rushing back.

Funny thing was, very few of them were happy. Though she supposed that had a lot to do with the fact she rarely allowed herself to be happy back then. Given how she'd been living the past five years and how different her life was, the thought broke her heart a little. She'd never noticed it back then, but after experiencing a joyful life, she wasn't sure she could go back to a life like her old one.

"I haven't," she said under her breath, glancing around for any hint as to where he might be.

Her eyes landed on a speaker built into the wall. So, the intercom system was in place before Justin got there. Maybe it was a way to communicate between the house and the barn, or maybe they'd had ranch hands at one point and this was the easier way to get messages to their staff. With any luck, it would be an older system, which would mean there was likely a dedicated room where a person would have to make the announcements from. New technology was definitely handy sometimes but could be a real pain in the ass to trace with all the Bluetooth and wireless and everything.

She eased down the wall, glad she had dark clothes on.

Her eyes were finally starting to adjust, and she spotted a wire running up a post in front of her. Tracing the wire with her eyes, she moved farther down the length of the barn, following it to a small room built into the back of the structure.

Silently she moved into position outside the door of the room, kicking it open, so ready to shoot. So ready for all this to be done.

But the room was empty.

"Aw, Sparrow, you didn't think it would be that easy, did you?" came the disembodied voice.

No, Ava thought, but she'd be lying that she hadn't hoped he'd be that careless and underestimating of her.

And now she knew he was watching her too. Hard to track someone when they had eyes on you, but you had absolutely no idea where they were. But it was dim inside the barn, the windows shuttered, the only light coming from the fires.

Ava moved quickly, ducking behind the nearest fire. If he was using infrared to track her, she would use his own fire trick against him. She moved again to the next nearest fire, then the next. It wouldn't be impossible to track her, but she was damn well going to make it as hard as she could.

The real problem was, she had no idea where the hell Justin even was. And he probably had her exact location pinpointed.

She closed her eyes…had to think. If she were Justin, where would she go?

And then, with the intuitive clarity that used to fuel her every move, honed over years in her former life, she knew.

Up.

Justin would be somewhere above, in the loft. Advantage was at the high ground where you can see your enemy coming. Usually. She had to figure a way to go up without waltzing right into some trap he'd no doubt set for her. She desperately needed an advantage of her own. *She* needed the higher ground.

A quick glance around told her there were several ladders leading to the hayloft, and she'd bet her life each one of them was booby-trapped somehow. And if she knew Justin, those traps would do harm, yes, but it would not be enough to kill her—only to weaken her so he could toy with her some more.

Coward.

But Ava didn't need to get to the loft. She needed to get higher. She needed to get to the roof.

Of course, getting onto the roof of a barn was not an easy task considering a two-story barn was usually thirty feet up, and this one was no exception. She also needed to get there without Justin knowing what she was up to.

She needed a distraction.

And as the final rays of sun shone through the edges of the shuttered windows, the dust dancing around as it passed through the sun streaks, an idea started to form. Dust. So much dust. Highly flammable dust if given the proper variables.

And she'd passed a bunch of yard and lawn tools on her way into the barn that would come in very handy, indeed. Bags of grain lay stacked against the nearest stall. The feed looked like it had been there for a long time, as if the animals the grain had been intended for had been gone awhile and no one ever got around to getting rid of it. If Ava were very lucky, maybe the grain had even begun to form the dusty black mold that was very bad for a person to breathe in, but that would be perfect for her plan.

Ava crept back to the pile of yard tools and pulled out what she needed. The gas-powered leaf blower wasn't going to be quiet, but if her plan worked it wouldn't matter if Justin knew where she was.

Because she would not be there for long.

Making her way back to the sacks of grain, Ava pulled out the small knife from its sheath near her boot and made a long, quick slice down the front of each stack. Grain began to leak out. She put her knife away and pushed the primer button a few times before yanking the cord. It made a hideous sound, no doubt instantly alerting Justin to her location.

She pulled the cord again, and again—hideous sound, no start.

Scrambling came from above, and she knew she'd only get one more chance.

She yanked that damn cord with every ounce of

strength she had and the thing finally, blessedly, roared to life.

In one swift move, Ava kicked over the stacks of grain, causing a huge plume of dust to billow into the air as she pointed the leaf blower toward its destination—the nearest fire, and on the other side of it, a nice, convenient stack of hay, dry and brittle, and best of all, gloriously flammable.

It hadn't been Justin's best move to light those fires, Ava thought as she ran in the opposite direction toward one of the shuttered windows.

Even though they were behind her, Ava knew the flames were huge. The heat was heavy at her back, and as she scrambled the few feet to the window and pushed the shutter open, she risked a glance back and smiled as the flames licked their way around the edges of the haystack.

It wouldn't keep Justin busy forever, but if he had some master plan to deal with her in the loft, he'd have to put out the fire first. Footsteps pounded on wood somewhere deep inside the barn and Ava knew she was right.

She flung one leg over the windowsill, then eased to the ground on the other side, gently closing the shutter behind her.

Problem one down. Now there was just the little matter of how to get onto the roof of the exceedingly tall, and extremely daunting—now that she was getting a good look at it—building. She ran a full circle around the barn, pleased to see a bit of smoke billowing from the east side—Justin was no doubt losing his shit, which made her extremely happy—but there was no obvious way up the structure.

Scratch that.

There was one very obvious way, but Ava really did not want to take it. Unfortunately, there were no trees, or any structures around that might be hiding a handy-dandy ladder that might happen to reach all the way to the roof either, so it made her decision easy.

The decision was easy, but the execution definitely wouldn't be. Back when she was in the field, she might not give too much thought to it, but now that she'd let herself…soften for five years, she was not sure how this was going to go.

Off the front of the barn, there was a pulley system that must have once been used to transport feed, or hay, or who knew what up to the second floor of the barn. The heavy metal contraption was bolted above the sec-ond-floor door, close to the roof.

Ava took a deep breath and let it out in a big, de-termined whoosh. It was now or never, she knew, and jumped up onto the long rope dangling near the ground. Inch by inch she eased up the rope, moving hands above her head, then pushing with her legs, trying her damned-est not to look down. But the moment she had that pesky thought that she should not look down, the task, of course, became impossible.

Halfway up, Ava began to think the whole thing had been a very bad idea. Her arms, not used to the kind of stress, began to shake, but she tried to kind of zone out, to keep moving and not think too much. Eventually she made it to the heavy metal wheel part of the pulley and above it, the strong wooden post, about six inches square. She hadn't thought this next part all the way through. She was only taking it one step at a time, and with her arms as weak and spent as they were, she wasn't sure she could hoist herself up to the post. Although, given the situation she was in, so high from the ground, she wasn't entirely sure she could make it back down either, so again, easy decision…and a difficult execution.

She tried to visualize her plan. Maybe she could kick her feet up and go legs first, but the thought of dangling upside down made her shove that idea away pretty quickly. She honestly still didn't know if it was going to work when she decided to simply go for it, moving her legs up close under her, gripping the rope with her feet and pushing herself partway above the post, steadying herself by grasping the post and heaving her way the final few inches.

As she straddled the post, her heart raced, and everything else shook, and then, even worse, she accidentally looked down. A little zip of wooziness forced her to scramble up over the edge of the roof to its relative safety faster than she could say giddyap.

Which was definitely also faster than she could process that she just climbed to the roof of a barn that was, you know, on fire.

But a girl couldn't have everything. One step at a time was about all a person could handle in a situation where their ex-boyfriend slash stalker slash attempted murderer is after them and everyone they love.

Legs still shaking, Ava made her way to the first of two little vent stacks with the cute tiny roofs on the top of the barn. She supposed they had a name but had absolutely no idea what it might be. And absolutely no desire to care, what with the whole burning building beneath her and everything. Which was when she decided to risk a peek, leaning a bit toward the east side of the barn. There was smoke, but it didn't seem any worse than before, and since it wasn't streaming out of the vent she was currently leaning on, she figured Justin must have it under control. It would have been pretty careless to light a bunch of fires inside an old dusty barn filled with hay and not have a few extinguishers lying around.

The slats in the vent stack allowed Ava a bit of a view back into the barn. It was almost as dark in there as it was becoming outside, the last whispers of light melting into darkness as she rested, knowing that what had gotten her this far had been the easy part.

And then a shadow crossed as she watched, a darkness breaking the muted orange of the glowing fires. The path of the shadow was determined, confident, not evading or using maneuvers to try to stay hidden. Either Justin was very sure of his plan, or he had no idea about her perch above.

He moved fast, and almost instantly past where she could see, heading for the back of the barn. Ava got up and hung on to the vent stack as she eased around it. The roof was steeply pitched, but she was surprised at how steady she felt up there. Though she supposed anything would feel steady after the monstrous climb of doom she'd just performed.

Careful of making noise, Ava made her way down the roof, stepping carefully in the dark, testing each step before putting her full weight on it. It was an old barn, but it was sturdy, and she made it to the second vent stack in a minute or so.

Jackpot.

Justin wasn't directly below the vent, but he was in

her line of vision. Surrounded by monitors and electronic equipment, the guy had a whole intelligence center going on right inside that rustic old barn. She should
have known. Justin wasn't one to trust his instincts, always preferring the backup of technology to show him
the easiest way.

And then on one of the screens, she saw something.
A man, wandering through the house, and she couldn't
help herself—her body moving of its own accord—when
she leaned in a bit further to get a better look.

And that's when she heard the big crack.

But she didn't have time to figure out where it was
coming from before the world in front of her gave way,
the vent falling in on itself.

Which was precisely when she began to plummet.

Zach knew only two things. He had to get to Chloe,
then he had to get to Ava. He had absolutely no idea
how he was going to do either of those things, but he
was going to damn well do them anyway.

The screens flashed again, and Chloe's face appeared. She was somewhere dark. The grainy gray feed
of Chloe's face looked like night vision, but the sun was
still peeking out over the horizon, the setting sun coating everything in a sickly pink glow.

Which meant there weren't any windows wherever
she was.

His guts started to churn. What if she wasn't in the
house at all? Or anywhere on the property? The bastard
had moved her at least once, even if it was stopping only
long enough to take a picture at the old hunting shack.

But Zach knew he had no choice. He had to search

every inch of the property because, well, frankly he had no other option. So he began to search, knowing full well it was an exercise in frustration and he was going to descend further and further into panic the entire time.

The screens flashed once more and Zach trained his eyes on Chloe, studying every inch of the screen for some kind of clue to let him know where she might be. And then he saw it. A small circle a bit brighter than the rest of the feed, as if a tiny bit of sun was trying to break through. A knot in a piece of wood, maybe? Or even a crack? But before the screen switched again, Zach knew one small thing more than he did before. He'd had frenzied visions of underground spaces, bunkers, panic rooms impossible to get into, but now he knew she was in a space where there must be at least one window—a covered window, but a window nonetheless.

Zach took a big breath and screamed, "Chloe!"

He'd forgotten where he was and a wave of dizziness washed over him, making him thrust an arm out to grab the wall, nearly falling. He moved back out of the closet, stepping over the police officer and wondering how deadly the gas was. But the thought pushed to the back of his mind as he stumbled toward the door of the bedroom.

"Chloe!" he yelled again, the effort forcing him to pause and lean on the doorframe.

His vision swirled for a moment, then righted itself, like the worst head rush of his life. As long as the effects weren't permanently affecting him, he was damn well going to use every moment he had to get to his daughter.

He moved back toward the living room. There was a chance Chloe could be in the basement, and he wasn't about to leave the place without exhausting every possible chance he had at finding her.

As another wave of dizziness rolled through, his head feeling heavier, his body moving slower, his thoughts getting thicker, he made his way to the large windows. If the gas was this potent, and if there was any chance Chloe was anywhere nearby, he needed to air the place out. He thought about going back and closing the bedroom door the gas was coming from, but if there was any chance Banyan was still alive, he couldn't do that. The officer had clearly already been through a hell of a lot. Judging from the headache already threatening to strangle Zach's efforts at finding Chloe and Ava, if the officer did wake up, he was going to be suffering, and Zach couldn't bear to make that even worse.

He struggled with the old windows that clearly hadn't been opened for a while, but finally got the crank to move the tiniest bit. After another lurch or two, the window gave way, a whoosh of fresh air pouring in, aided by the window he'd climbed through on the other side of the room. He repeated the effort with one more window, then moved toward the basement stairs, which he'd seen near the entrance.

The stairwell was dim, but even as he was descending, Zach could already sense this wasn't going to be where he found Chloe. The light from the stairway would have illuminated the feed from the camera more, he was sure of it, but he supposed, in his hazy stupor, it was possible there could be a room built down there that was darker.

The sensation as he made his way down the stairs was similar to being drunk, with brief moments of clarity alternating with bouts of fogginess through which he concentrated hard, trying to find lucidity again. And then, without fully knowing how he'd gotten there, he was standing in the middle of an empty room, light streaming in through windows on all sides.

Chloe was nowhere to be found.

Still, Zach fumbled to open every door in that basement. He wasn't sure in the end how many there were, it felt like a hundred, but even he knew that didn't make sense.

He blinked a few times and shook his head, which seemed to help a little, then made his way back up the stairs to the main floor. The task took far more exertion than it should have, but he got the sense the toxin was already weaker than before, and maybe he was on the other side of it. His head still felt like it was in a vise and his eyelids were heavier than ever, but the fresh air as he crested the top of the stairs helped even more.

"Chloe!" he yelled one more time before reaching for the doorknob to leave.

He had no idea what his plan was, but he'd exhausted every possible hiding place in the house.

But as he turned the knob, a clunk sounded. A clunk from somewhere inside the house.

"Chloe?" he yelled again, this time more questioning, his heart starting to beat a little faster.

The clunk sounded again, and this time Zach was ready for it, listening intently for where it was coming from.

The ceiling?

It took Zach far longer than it should have to figure it out. How could he have been so dense?

The attic.

Zach figured it must be the gas, or at least that was the story he was going with as he stumble-ran through the house searching for an access panel. Living room, nothing. Kitchen nothing…he went through the bedrooms, even stepping over the police officer to peek into the closet of horrors, but still nothing until he reached the back bedroom on the left, tucked away inside the closet, where he finally found what he was looking for.

"Chloe, I'm coming!" he yelled, then ran back to the kitchen for a chair, positioning it under the panel and sliding it open.

But even with the chair he was still too far below the opening to see inside. With the still-foggy brain, Zach didn't know where he summoned the strength—it must have been pure adrenaline—but somehow, he jumped and pulled himself partway through the small hole, and still half hanging out, he scanned the dark space.

A scurrying noise came from somewhere in the shadows, and Zach braced himself once more.

But it wasn't an enemy to fight that he saw. It was his amazing Chloe—hands tied and a cloth around her mouth—but otherwise looking healthy and uninjured.

Relief flooded him, and he didn't even care how much he shook with the effort of hanging there as his daughter looped her arms around his neck and began to cry.

Chapter 19

Everything hurt.

Ava started to move slowly, trying—unsuccessfully—not to groan, unsure as to what might be injured or broken...or what might be coming at her next. Eventually she rolled onto her back, and nothing seemed to be broken, but her muscles screamed. This was going to hurt tomorrow.

If she made it to tomorrow.

A slow clap started from somewhere in the rafters. "You always did know how to make an entrance," Justin said.

Ava couldn't see where he was, exactly, but from the direction of his voice, she got the general idea of his whereabouts being ahead of her and to her right. She had seen him just before her fall though, so he couldn't have gotten far.

"Asshole," she said under her breath, realizing—as she picked a few splinters of wood from her shirt—that he had to have doctored the vent stack, set it to crumble.

The first one she leaned against had been as strong as the day it was built, but the second folded in on itself like the origami game she used to play as a kid to determine her future. She was still waiting on her "large fortune" and "many cats."

"I have to say, you've played into my plan exactly as you were supposed to," his voice said, faraway and tinny.

A speaker.

He'd known exactly what she was going to do before she did it. Of course, he'd had the advantage of time—scoping out the property and putting measures in place to ensure she did what he expected. She wondered if he'd even bothered to booby-trap the ladders or if he knew she'd assume they'd been tampered with.

Ava began to realize one thing. In the time she'd been slowly getting to her feet, Justin could have taken her out six times. But that wasn't what he wanted. He wanted to toy with her. To make her suffer—both physically and mentally. He wanted to control her.

And she hated that she'd played right into his game. Her face burned…with rage, embarrassment, she wasn't sure. Probably a combination of both. She used to be better than this.

She needed to be better than this.

"Where's Chloe?" she spat, wiping at the bit of blood on her lip.

"She's safe," Justin said. "Might take a while for that…gentleman of yours to find her though."

Of course. Justin would do everything in his power to keep Zach busy. To keep him away while he played out his sick game. To have Ava all to himself. To do what he failed at the first time.

But Ava wasn't going to make it easy. If it was a choice between saving herself or saving Zach and Chloe, it wasn't a choice. She'd gladly sacrifice for them, and she was prepared. But if there was a chance, a way to keep the life she'd built…well, she was going to bloody well try for it. And lucky for her, she didn't care about teaching anyone any lessons, or whatever the hell it was Justin was trying to do or prove. The first chance she got she would take him out. No questioning, no overthinking, no excuses. She reached behind her back for her gun.

Shit.

It must have dislodged in the fall. Ava glanced back to the pile of rubble wondering if it was worth trying to find, when a shadow jumped out at her. Except, of course, it wasn't just a shadow. It was the man she hoped she'd never see again. She was caught off guard, knocked to the floor, tumbling, tangling with him. She never wanted to be this close to him again. Had fiery, burning nightmares about it after the bunker explosion.

But as they rolled once more, Ava realized something. All those years spent worrying about Justin finding her, terrified about what might happen, were for nothing. In fact, now that he'd found her, she realized it was the best thing that could ever happen.

Because truly, this was the only way to end it.

She wrapped one leg around Justin's waist and used the momentum of the roll to heave herself to the top position. Justin anticipated the move and countered, but it was enough to untangle them and send her scrambling a few feet away.

Justin got to his feet quickly, but so did Ava, finally coming face-to-face with the man who'd very nearly killed her five years ago.

"Good to see you, Sparrow," he said, the words not so much being spoken as they were oozing out of him.

"Afraid I can't say the same," Ava said, "though it is a little alarming to see you this way."

"Scared?" he asked.

Ava scoffed. "I meant your appearance is alarming, not the situation," she said.

Justin had always been vain, and Ava knew how to hit him where it hurt. He was an attractive person, most spies were—it helped their marks trust them—and he would still be considered handsome. But he had definitely aged, and Ava wasn't above using any tactic she could to get inside his head.

His eye twitched and she knew she was on the right track, but then he smiled.

They were giving each other a wide berth, circling the loft of the barn. Ava's hands were out at the ready, as were Justin's, though he clearly had the advantage, considering the knife in his hand.

"It has been a long five years," he said, as if shrugging the comment off, but Ava knew better.

"Really?" she said, as if she didn't have a care in the world. "Because they've been the absolute best five years of my life."

She wasn't lying either…she'd give anything to go back to her warm little Ambrosia Falls house and be quite content for the rest of time. She'd kind of fallen into being an operative in the first place. It was cliché, a recruiter singling her out in college, citing her advanced marks and athletic abilities, but even then, Ava knew her desirability as an agent had more to do with the fact that she didn't have any close family left, or many other connections for that matter.

Ugh, and she hated to admit it, but all that was probably how Justin had been able to get close to her too. Once someone became an operative, they couldn't live a normal life anymore. It was inevitable that operatives tended to attract each other like magnets…it was really the only way to have a relationship at all.

Of course, there was a whole lot of risk in getting involved with an agent, which Ava knew as well as anybody, she just never thought she'd be gullible enough to fall for it. Which was, of course, her real mistake. Believing she was smarter than Justin…less gullible. Except she'd been the one who got played. She supposed it was inevitable, this instinct to continue assuming she was smarter than him—everyone believed they were smarter than everyone else in the room most of the time. But she wasn't about to underestimate him again.

She would, however, do her damnedest to make sure he thought she'd become a whole lot weaker than she had. Her limp, as she moved slowly, never taking her eyes off Justin, was real, but she might have been exaggerating it…just a little. Maybe more than a little. She swiped at her lip again, reminding Justin of the cut he put there with his clever, clever ways.

"Looks like it hurts," Justin said, a gleam in his eye that Ava decidedly did not like.

It was a little too wild, a little too unhinged.

"It's fine," she said, though she didn't try to sell the point too much.

As she said it, Justin lunged, knife hand out. He was trying to catch her off guard again, trying to make her duck to the left, which would have sent her tumbling over the edge of the loft, but she was too well-trained. Ava didn't even have to try to memorize the details of her surroundings anymore, it happened automatically, and instinct thrust her in the opposite direction.

They continued to circle, Ava watching Justin's eyes, his hands…every twitch of every muscle, her mind working, trying to come up with a plan. She was moving toward the rubble of the vent stack, her gun at the forefront of her mind. She had no doubt Justin had a gun on him somewhere too, but it would likely be hard to get it, and he wouldn't pull it out unless she had one too. He wanted a fair fight. He'd been beaten by Ava before, and his tiny ego wouldn't allow for him to win at a disadvantage. He'd have to win fair and square.

Her feet slid across the floor, the dirt and hay and splintered bits of woods dampening the sound of their footfalls.

She was beginning to form a tiny inkling of a plan. It was a terrible plan, but it was all she had. It was too much to hope she'd happen upon her gun, but if she could get to one of the sharp splinters of wood, one large enough to do a little damage if embedded in the right appendage at the right angle, she could have a chance. Of course, that was a lot of ifs. If she saw an appropriate piece…if she was able to get a hold of it…if she was able to get close enough to Justin to do some damage. But it was what she had. He wasn't going to wait around all day before he made another move.

Justin lunged for her, a flame from one of his fires glinting off the blade, and Ava put her plan into motion. She ducked, rolling along her right shoulder, grabbing as much debris from the floor as her hand would hold as she went. She jumped back to her feet and spun to face him, checking her treasures. There was a single splinter that might do, and as she discarded the rest, she made her own lunge toward Justin, driving the splinter home with all her might, but at the last second, he saw it coming and turned, just enough for the wood to dig into his shoulder instead of closer to his chest where she'd been aiming.

Justin let out an animalistic wail, clearly injured, but also clearly even more pissed off now as his eyes went wild and he came straight for her.

Ava had no time to react as he hit her full-on with his entire weight, sending them both toward the railing of the loft area. The wood railing only crackled for a second before it gave way, sending them into free fall, a sensation Ava had hoped she wouldn't experience again, let alone so soon. Though maybe because she'd already been through this once in the past few minutes, she was less caught off guard than Justin seemed to be. His wild eyes filled with fear. She swung a leg around his body and used the momentum to spin them both, hoping like hell he would be the one to hit the floor first.

Zach lifted his precious cargo down from the attic and set her on the floor. He was as gentle as he could be as he bent down and removed the cloth from around her mouth and cut the rope free from her hands.

Even though she hadn't done it in years, Chloe scurried up and clung onto his neck, not letting go even when he stood, ignoring the slice of pain shooting though his leg. Pain was nothing, not when he finally had his daughter back.

He moved back down the hall carrying his only child,

and tears filled his eyes when Chloe whispered, "I knew you'd come."

He held her close as he continued to stumble toward the door, realizing for the first time he hadn't thought about what he might do when he found Chloe. They had no truck to retreat to, no safe space to go to figure out their next move.

Suddenly, Chloe stiffened. "What's wrong, Dad?"

She pulled back and looked at him, alarm filling her eyes.

"Nothing's wrong anymore, sweetheart," he said, taking another step toward the door.

"Dad," Chloe scolded. "What's wrong with your leg? You shouldn't be carrying me."

"I don't want to let you go," he said, continuing to stumble along.

"Dad!" she said, louder this time. "Stop. Put me down. Please."

Zach didn't want to admit it, but his leg *was* making it a whole lot more difficult to rescue Chloe. He didn't want to be hurt, he didn't want to admit it was hampering the whole "brave, strong dude" thing he had going on, but he wasn't some sort of superhero. He was just a guy who would do anything for his kid.

"It's okay, Chloe," Zach said.

"Dad," Chloe said, her tone more serious than a veteran teacher dealing with the school bully for the fourth time that semester. "Put. Me. Down."

Zach eased Chloe out of his arms as gingerly as he could, trying not to wince. "I want to make sure you're okay."

"Yeah, same," she said, putting her hands on her hips.

A little pang of something—sadness that she was growing up so fast, maybe—shot through him, but he knew this was the real Chloe. The very capable, caring and concerned kid he wasn't quite sure how he raised to be so amazing, and so completely herself.

"I'll be fine," he said, trying not to let his limp betray his words.

Chloe side-eyed him like she knew he was full of it, which he absolutely was. The truth was, his leg hurt like hellfire pokers were twisting around in there, but his job wasn't done yet, so he wasn't about to stop and try to do something about it.

"Come on," he said, leading her toward the door. "We need to figure out what to do next."

"We have to get Ava and get out of here," Chloe said matter-of-factly, as if the whole thing was obvious.

"How did you know Ava was here?"

"*He* kept talking about her," Chloe said, the word coming out like she had a bad taste in her mouth. "It was so annoying. And then he started calling her some dumb bird name." She thought for a moment. "Sparrow, I think. It was so weird. He is *so* weird."

Zach marveled at how even a kidnapping could do little to keep Chloe's feistiness at bay. "That's one word for it, I guess," he said.

Chloe smiled conspiratorially like she knew a few other choice words her dad might prefer to call the guy.

"Okay, you're right. Ava is out here, and I have to find her, but first I need to find someplace safe for you."

"I can come with you—" Chloe started to say, but Zach put up a hand to cut her off.

"There is no way that is happening," he said in the

tone of voice he hated to use, but under the circumstances, it was warranted.

Chloe sighed. "Fine." The word came out with a little pout, but Zach knew she wasn't going to argue.

He hoped to hell that tone was never going to stop working on the poor kid, no matter how much it hurt him to have to use it, since he had no idea what he would do if he didn't have it in his arsenal.

Zach unlocked, then opened the door slowly, peeking out first to make sure the coast was clear. He had an idea in the back of his mind, one that made a lot of sense, but something didn't feel quite right about it. Still, he and Chloe crept out of the house, and after looking in every direction, moved quickly toward the edge of the trees. His instincts screamed at him to run, but something held him back.

They made it to the tree line, and after about eight more feet, Zach stopped.

"What are we doing?" Chloe whispered.

"I don't know," Zach whispered back.

He glanced around again, then headed in the same direction. A few yards more and he stopped. He looked at Chloe.

"What?" she asked, knowing something was up.

He leaned back on a fallen log to give his leg a bit of a rest. As he looked at Chloe, whose eyes were wide with concern and questioning, he decided to be honest.

"I don't know what to do," he said.

"Okay," Chloe replied, as if she had expected as much.

"It's just... I know where there's a place that should be safe, and you'd be sheltered and out of harm's way."

"Okaaaay," Chloe said again, this time dragging the word out as if to say, *spit it out, Dad.*

Zach sighed. "But something doesn't feel right about it."

Chloe shrugged. "So, we don't go there. You always have to trust your instincts, Dad."

The kid was right. Thinking about taking Chloe to the cop car should have been a no-brainer, but visions of his own truck blowing up sent shivers down his spine. If anyone had been even close to the truck when it went... well, he didn't even want to think about that.

He nodded once. "You're right," he said.

He had, after all, always taught Chloe exactly that—trust your gut.

"I don't know where you'll be safe. And I need to know you're safe."

Chloe looked around. "What about right there?" she said, motioning with her hand to exactly where he was sitting.

"With me?" Zach asked, wishing for nothing more than to be able to do exactly that and keep her with him for eternity, but he couldn't leave Ava.

"No," Chloe said, delivering another magnificent eye roll, "under the log you're sitting on."

Zach shifted, looking over his shoulder. The ground was covered in tall fernlike vegetation that would provide almost total cover.

"I can hide in the space under there."

It was pretty brilliant. Still, Zach was hesitant. "What if there are bugs under there?" he asked.

She looked up at him through her lashes, very much

not impressed. "I am not the one who is afraid of bugs," she said, shaking her head the tiniest bit.

Right. Right, it was absolutely him that did not love the creepy-crawlies.

Like, at all.

"What about rain?" he asked.

Chloe squinted up at sky—what little of it she could see through the trees—and stitched a "seriously?" kind of look onto her face. "There aren't even any clouds. And besides, I'll be under a log, the rain isn't going to get me."

"It could seep down under there," Zach said, raising an eyebrow as if daring her to challenge his logic.

"Um, so I guess my butt will get a little wet then," she said, shooting him an "are we done this ridiculous argument yet" look, already starting to crawl under the log.

Zach stood and tested the fallen tree trunk to make sure it was sturdy and wasn't about to fall on her head or anything, but the thing felt like it was stuck there with concrete.

"Fine," he said. "But you need to stay right here."

Chloe nodded.

"I am so serious, Chloe. After everything, can you imagine what would happen if I come back here and you're gone?"

Chloe peeked out from the log. "I'm guessing your head would pop right off."

And the way she said it—so grim—Zach couldn't help but bark out a laugh. "That is exactly correct. My head would pop off and that would be the end of me."

Chloe's face softened but was still serious. "I'm not going anywhere, Dad. I promise."

"Okay," he said, knowing she was telling the truth.

"Just stay here, stay quiet. I don't know, try to sleep or something, and I'll be back as soon as I can."

"Don't worry about me, Dad," she said, as Zach leaned over to plant a kiss on the top of her head. "I'm getting pretty used to entertaining myself."

Zach smiled, but as he stood, a pang of sorrow whooshed through him. The poor kid had been kidnapped and left to essentially fend for herself. Nothing to keep her mind busy, and here she was pretty much taking care of him.

And there he was, leaving her all alone again.

"I will be back soon," he said, turning before she could see the glistening in his eyes.

After everything she'd been through, the last thing Chloe needed was to be worried about him.

Chapter 20

The good news was, the landing had forced the jagged stake all the way through the fleshy part of Justin's shoulder so it poked through to the other side. The not so good news was—as Ava blinked, another round of pain shooting through her body—she noticed her eye was about half an inch from being impaled on said piece of wood.

Unfortunately, Justin noticed too.

He twisted his body, trying to move the stake farther toward Ava's head as her eyes snapped shut and she felt the heavy graze of the wood across her eyelid.

Justin rolled as he twisted, trying to get the upper hand, but with his injured shoulder he was sluggish, and as he moved above her, Ava took advantage of the momentum to maneuver her foot into his torso and kick him away. She scrambled to her feet quickly, at the same time Justin also righted himself.

As they faced off yet again, Ava spoke.

"It doesn't have to be this way, Justin. I'm not in the business anymore. Whoever you were working for—the people who wanted me gone—don't matter anymore. I'm no threat to anybody out here."

Justin plastered on a wild smile. "Sounds exactly like

someone who was trying to pretend they had a nice, quiet life in the boonies would say."

They continued to move slowly, circling again, though they were both moving slower, and with decidedly more effort than before.

Ava sighed. "I'm not working anymore, Justin. If I was, you would have heard about it by now."

"There are plenty of jobs that have been unclaimed or unaccounted for over the past five years. A surprising amount, really. And this place," he said, motioning around him, though Ava knew he meant the entire area of Ambrosia Falls, "is a perfect cover. Remote. No one questioning your comings and goings."

"I live in a small town, Justin," Ava said. "Everyone knows my comings and goings. Believe me, Ambrosia Falls is not a place one can easily keep their business to themselves."

Justin shrugged. "Maybe…maybe not. Either way, my employers are not willing to take that chance." He paused for a moment, as if mulling over whether he should say the next part. Apparently, he decided to go for it. "Besides, I've been waiting way too long for this moment to walk away now."

Ava wasn't surprised. She knew this had long been personal for Justin, even if her emotions over him, other than anger, had ended ages ago.

"I'm sorry to hear that," Ava said in the most impersonal tone she could muster. Nothing frustrated Justin more than not being taken as seriously as he wanted. Sure, the situation was certainly serious, but Ava was going to try damn hard to make Justin think he meant nothing to her. Which, if he hadn't been literally in her face, would be true. "It's going to be tedious having to deal with you."

Justin squinted at her, and Ava knew he was trying to formulate a comeback. She used the moment to lunge for him, aiming toward his bad shoulder. If that piece of wood hurt going in, it was going to burn like the rage of a teen with a bad attitude being pushed back out. She balled her fist and impacted him with the fleshy, outside part of her hand. The wood sliced into her a little, but it was nothing compared to the way it sliced back through Justin, his wail confirming it was not an overly pleasant experience.

Ava desperately needed her gun, but she couldn't be sure Justin hadn't set traps on the ladders, and knowing Justin, if an incendiary of some sort had been set, it wouldn't just be a simple flash-bang to scare someone off. It would do some damage.

She couldn't risk it.

But Justin was already gathering himself, and she needed time to think. She turned and fled down a corridor in the barn, a wall on one side and a row of animal stalls on the other. She considered ducking into one of the stalls, but once inside, she'd be trapped, so she kept running.

"Sparrooow," Justin called, dragging the word out, and it was just like him to be all creepy, as if he were the evil star of his very own horror movie.

What an egotistical ass.

Ava rounded the corner of the passage, making her way back into the main area of the barn, the fires still burning around the room, the heat stifling, an eerie red glow making the whole place seem like it was simmering in a bath of embers.

Ducking and using each firepit as cover, Ava made her way back toward the pile of yard tools she'd found the leaf blower in, and tried to quietly grab something she could use as a weapon. While she successfully managed to get her hands on a simple garden rake, she'd made a god-awful clatter—loud enough to raise the devil himself, which was actually pretty fitting, given her surroundings.

She wheeled around, sure Justin would be right behind her, but he was still a bit of a distance away, just coming around the corner of the passage he followed her through.

Justin smirked in a kind of "aw, isn't that cute" kind of way, looking sadly at her rake.

What a cocky jackass, she thought, and since the rake was all Ava had, she moved toward Justin, wanting nothing more than to end this. But as she made her way across the room, Justin slowly and deliberately reached out his good arm, grabbing hold of a tool of his own that had been conveniently leaning against the wall, hidden behind a few bales of hay. Which, she realized, he'd probably planted there earlier.

A gleaming, and rather sharp-looking pitchfork.

Ava glanced around the massive space, wondering what other items might be conveniently hidden around the place. Not that she had much time to think about it, since she hadn't stopped moving even when Justin pulled out the damn giant fork.

She just needed to be better than him, that was all there was to it. And yeah, maybe she'd let her training lapse a little in the past few years, and yeah, Justin had probably done the opposite, biding his time by honing his skills, but she was still confident. She'd always been better than him. At least that's what she was telling herself, even if a tiny voice somewhere deep in her head was whispering to her consciousness with inklings of doubt.

And maybe it was the doubt that got her. Threw her off her game, because as she neared Justin, something about the glint of the pitchfork distracted her. Or maybe it was the look on Justin's face, like he had so much hatred for her and honestly, Ava didn't know why. Didn't know what she'd ever done to him besides bring him close and make a life with him.

Ava raised her rake. It felt far too flimsy in her hands, far too old and maybe even ready to break, but it was all she had, and she brought it down hard, aiming for Justin's head, sure it wouldn't knock him unconscious, but maybe, if she was lucky, it might do some kind of brief damage. She imagined her follow-through might skim past the nasty gash on his shoulder, but as it turned out, there was no follow-through.

Only two tines of a pitchfork settling neatly and deeply into her forearm as her hands were raised above her head.

The pain was inconceivable. Ava had been hurt before—it had been an inevitability in her past life—but this was breath-stealing, instant agony, the sharp metal piercing straight through her already burned arm. She yanked back in reaction, the tines coming free, but then the blood began to race from her body as if it were being chased from within, pouring to the floor.

Ava tried to run, tried to put pressure on the wounds to staunch the blood and buy some time—it needed to be stopped or, well, Ava didn't want to think about that—but Justin was ready, yanking her back by her hair and throwing her to the ground, straddling himself on top of her.

And then his hands were around her throat. She didn't know how he still possessed so much strength—his injured shoulder should have made it impossible to even move his arm, but he must have been running on pure adrenaline as he squeezed with both hands, the right one doing most of the work.

Ava tried to move beneath him, struggled to bring a leg up and shift him off her, but he was too strong.

Her thoughts became cloudy, and then suddenly the only thing she could focus on was Justin. She didn't want to give him the satisfaction—it was exactly what he wanted—but it was his eyes. Eyes that held so much in them, a wild, possessive rage. A fury fueled by years of failure and obsession and need to destroy…by the embarrassment of having lost once, and a vow it would never happen again.

Then, as the world started to pull in from the edges of her vision, a darkness taking its place, the look changed to something else.

Joy. Pleasure in the fact that he had won.

Ava closed her eyes. She couldn't watch the sick satisfaction washing over his features.

And then, a magnificent, unholy clunk reverberated through the air, and the weight on top of her shifted as her world faded to black.

The shovel felt heavy in his hands. He'd never once wanted to hurt someone like that, but seeing Justin choking Ava, Zach didn't think, he just reacted.

As he shoved the unconscious Justin to the floor, Zach was shocked at how pale Ava looked. Almost lifeless.

He moved quickly to her side, leaning his head close, listening for her breathing.

At first, he heard nothing, but then, the faintest flutter of air moved through her lips, and it was like his whole body exhaled. And that's when he felt it. Something wet soaking into his jeans, and even though the fires were going, the barn was still pretty dim, and he could only see whatever it was, was dark, almost black. He swiped at the stuff and his hands came away red, his stomach clenching.

Instantly, Zach noticed Ava's arm was covered in it too, and he knew he had to move fast—there was so much blood. He pulled his outer shirt off and wrapped it as tightly as he could around Ava's forearm, hoping with everything he had in him that it would be enough. After everything they'd been through, he couldn't lose her now.

He picked her up, the burning in his leg a constant reminder this was not an okay situation, and with one last glance at the lifeless-looking Justin, he hurried out of the barn and into the cool night air, only then realizing he didn't know how he was going to get her out of there. His truck was long gone, and he couldn't trust the police car.

But… Justin must have gotten out into the woods somehow, Zach realized, rushing toward the house, and its attached garage. The main door on the garage was locked, so he headed to the front door of the house. The garage was connected through the front entrance and

Zach made his way there quickly, elated to see a small SUV parked neatly in the center. He flung open the passenger seat and set Ava in as gently as he could, though a small moan wisped past her lips, which was both relieving and a little scary at the same time.

But nothing was more of a relief than a quick glance at the ignition where the keys were dangling. Perhaps Justin was preparing for a quick getaway. He buckled her seat belt and shut Ava's door, running to the driver's side and pushing the button to open the garage door as he slid behind the wheel.

He hit the gas and backed out of the garage fast, simultaneously rolling down the window.

"Chloe!" he yelled, still moving backward, turning the wheel until the headlights hit the edge of the forest. "Chloe, we gotta go!"

Zach was nearly to the edge of the trees, readying to throw the vehicle into park and race back into the woods, but, bless her heart, Chloe was already running out, as if she'd been waiting for this moment all along.

She flung open the back door, scrambled inside, and had the door shut faster than Zach would have thought possible. Her seat belt was on in seconds.

As Zach hit the gas and headed out the winding driveway, he glanced at Chloe in the rearview mirror. "Have you been practicing that or something?"

Chloe shrugged a shoulder. "Maybe a little in my head while I was waiting for you to come back."

Zach shook his head in amazement.

"What? I had a lot of time to think and worry," Chloe said, sounding a little defensive.

It was around that time Chloe noticed Ava was not looking too hot in the passenger seat.

"Dad!" she said, alarmed. "Is she okay?"

Zach glanced back at Chloe again and hated the look he saw on her face—terror mixed with confusion. He wished he still had the innocent confusion of a kid, wondering how something so terrible could happen to a good person.

"I hope so," Zach said.

He wanted so badly to tell Chloe Ava would be fine, but the truth was, he had no idea. He had no medical training, and truthfully, he'd only done what he'd seen people do on TV to wrap her wound. He knew it had to be tight, but beyond that, he had no clue.

"I'm going to be fine," Ava croaked, surprising them both.

She hitched up a little in the seat and turned to face Chloe. "Your dad saved me."

Chloe smiled then. "Me too."

And Zach's whole being burst with an uncomfortable prickle of a thousand emotions coursing through him. Embarrassment. Pride. A sense of not being worthy. Of not feeling like he'd done anything special, and in fact, like he'd done everything all wrong.

But most of all he felt grateful to be sitting there with the two most important people in his world.

"I don't need a hospital," Ava said. "I can deal with all this."

"Of course you need a hospital," Zach said. "You've lost a lot of blood."

Ava shook her head. "I can manage at home," she said, and then she looked at him, the expression on her face serious, like she was trying to tell him something without telling him something.

Something she didn't want to say in front of Chloe.

And then, with his heart breaking in two, and wondering how many times a heart could break in one day, Zach understood. They couldn't go to the hospital. She couldn't be stuck in a hospital with Justin still out there. She'd be a sitting duck.

He cleared his throat. "Yeah, okay," he said. "We'll just head home."

He didn't dare glance back to see what he knew would be an even more confused look on the face of his daughter as the vehicle fell silent for the rest of the drive home.

"I'd like to help you with that," Zach said, pulling into his driveway.

He wondered if it was okay to park the strange SUV right there in plain sight, but it wasn't like Justin didn't know where they both lived anyway, so he wasn't sure what the point would be. Unless, of course, the police came looking…though something told him the car was clear of any connection with Justin or any suspicion of any kind, really.

"Yeah," Ava said, gingerly moving to release her seat belt.

Chloe—the one Zach had been worrying about the longest over the past…how long was it? A day? God, it felt so much longer than that—had already bounded out of the vehicle, as if completely unscathed by the whole ordeal. He didn't have any illusions that she wouldn't have some mental scars, but he was going to do everything in his power to make sure she had help, both professional and his own, in dealing with it all.

His first order of business was to be by Chloe's side as she crawled into bed, exhausted.

"Are you sure you don't want to talk about anything?" he asked, but Chloe shook her head. "I'm fine, Dad," she said, a "just leave it alone" tone to her voice. Clearly, she was not in the mood for some exhaustive rehash of everything right then.

Chloe gently pushed him out of her room so she could change—she was all about the privacy these days—and Ava met him in the hallway.

"You think she'll be okay?" he asked her.

He was the parent. He should have been the one to feel certain about what his daughter was feeling one way or the other, but he honestly had no clue. Why did all the other parents always seem like they knew exactly what they were doing? Were they all faking it too?

"Give yourself a break," Ava said, like she was reading his mind. "She'll be fine, and if she's not, the two of you are going to figure it out together."

Zach nodded, though he was far from convinced.

Chloe opened her door again and they both stepped inside as she crawled into bed.

"Think you'll be able to sleep?" Zach asked.

Chloe nodded. "I can barely keep my eyes open."

"Okay good," Zach said, then did something he hadn't done in years.

Turned on the old baby monitor he used when Chloe was little and hadn't gotten around to putting away yet. Although, truth be told, he'd still used it over the years without Chloe knowing about it. It was a habit he'd only stopped about a year ago, though he wished he hadn't.

Maybe he could have prevented this whole thing before it even started.

"Are you serious, Dad?" Chloe said, giving him a look that said she was not at all impressed.

"Just for tonight, okay?" Zach said. "I just need reassurance for right now."

Chloe sighed. "Fine, but we are not going to make a habit of this, right?" she asked, sounding more like she was the parent.

Zach smiled and stepped back while Ava sat on the bed. "Good night, sweet girl," she said, bending to kiss Chloe on the forehead.

"I'm glad you're okay," Chloe said.

Ava's eyes filled with tears then, and a thrum struck Zach's heart. Ava cared so much for Chloe, and Zach realized he would give anything to have this every night. Minus the abduction/explosions/revenge situation, obviously.

"I'm glad you're okay," Ava managed to whisper, booping Chloe on the nose.

She quickly got up and passed Zach as she left the room. He got the feeling she was trying to hide the extent of her emotions from them, but he wasn't fooled. Ava cared so much more than she would ever let on.

The only thing was, Zach couldn't figure out why she needed to hide anymore.

Ava was almost done rebandaging her arm by the time Zach limped back downstairs, the receiving end of the kid monitor in hand.

She was looking better after some water and clean bandages.

"You did a good job of this," she said, motioning to

her arm and the discarded pile of cloth. "Sorry about your shirt."

"I was worried it might be too tight," he said.

Ava shook her head. "It can never be too tight in a situation like this. More importantly, how's your leg?"

"I have no idea," Zach said, suddenly looking exhausted as he flopped into a chair. "I'm sure I'll live."

"After everything that leg has been through, we should check on the wound closure bandage."

Zach nodded and pulled his pants off, a sheepish look crossing his face. "I kind of hoped it would be different circumstances the first time I took my pants off in front of you," he said.

Ava let the corner of her mouth curl up in a half smile. "Me too."

But she went to work, not wanting to drag out a moment of Zach's pain longer than she had to.

"You should go into town for proper stitches tomorrow," she said, "but for now, this bandage is actually holding."

"Yeah okay," he said.

"And get some sleep," she told him, as she got up from her chair.

"Oh, um…right. Sleep. That's a thing," Zach said, his thoughts jumping all over the place.

He thought…hoped she might stay. It didn't seem right that they would, what? Just go their separate ways after everything? And yeah, maybe things had gotten intense between the two of them, but maybe he was reading too much into everything. Zach suddenly felt like a fool. He realized he'd built up everything in his head to be bigger than it was. They'd really only shared two kisses, after all, and had barely discussed what they even meant.

But she was his best friend, and two passionate kisses had to mean something.

Still, he supposed they could figure it all out tomorrow. He was pretty damn exhausted too.

She headed to the door, and on the porch, she turned back to Zach. "I'll see you tomorrow," she said, kissed him on the cheek and headed toward her house.

Chapter 21

Ava was not going to see Zach tomorrow. She wouldn't see him tomorrow, or on any other day in the near future.

Justin was still out there somewhere, and the only thing she could do now was run. He wouldn't have a way to inform her if he tried to go after Zach or Chloe again, no way to use them as leverage if she could get far enough, fast enough. He would leave them alone and come after her.

But it was going to be the hardest thing she'd ever done. Leaving them.

A tear rolled down her cheek as she climbed the steps to her front door and slipped inside, needing to gather a few things before she left Ambrosia Falls forever.

In less than half an hour, Ava was ready to go.

She took one last look around her house. It had been such a good house, everything she needed in a time where her whole world was imploding, and it had built her back up. Gave her back her life. No, gave her a brand-new life so much better than the one before, and damn it, she was going to miss the place. Which was a new feeling for her. She couldn't remember ever being attached to a place, not even as a kid. But this house, and Ambrosia Falls in general, were special places.

She could only hope the next people to live here would appreciate it as much as she did. She hoped they'd be nice. Zach and Chloe deserved to have great neighbors.

Ava flipped her living room light off for the last time, then turned to head out the door, jolting as she saw the dark figure in the open doorway. At first, it didn't compute. How had someone gotten the door open so quietly? But then she realized she'd left it unlocked. Even with all that was going on, she was slipping. So used to not having to lock her doors in the quiet little town, she'd done the same thing again, purely out of habit.

Cursing herself in her head, she readied to bolt in the other direction, when the figure spoke.

"You're leaving?"

They were just two little words, but they were filled with more emotion than Ava had ever heard in such a short phrase. Anger, confusion, disbelief, but most of all hurt. If a broken heart could stand up and talk, those two words were exactly what it might sound like.

"Zach," Ava whispered, unsure how to answer.

He stepped farther into the house, a stream of moonlight falling onto his face. In one hand he held the little walkie-talkie-like receiver from the baby monitor, which almost made Ava smile, and in the other hand he held…a letter?

Oh no.

"I was about to head to bed when I remembered. I'd been so caught up with Chloe missing and everything, I didn't have a chance to stop and wonder what the heck you were doing at my mailbox."

Ava swallowed, knowing she'd been exposed. That letter was supposed to be for later. For when she was gone.

"But then I was in the shower, and I remembered. You know, the way you always remember things when your mind finally has a chance to slow down and not think for a second, and then everything you missed during the day comes tumbling back at you?"

Ava nodded slowly. Her mind was whirling, panicked, dumbfounded. This wasn't the way things were supposed to go.

"I remembered a little flutter of a thought that something was weird about you standing out by my mailbox. There's nothing out there to see. Nothing to do. Just a mailbox." He held up the letter. "This is you leaving, isn't it?" he said, the crack in his voice giving away more than his face even, in the near darkness.

"I'm sorry," was all Ava could say, the words coming out in a whisper, and tears filled her eyes.

"You don't have to leave, Ava. You can't leave, not after this," he said, the letter shaking a little.

"I have to," Ava said, trying to pull her shoulders back, trying to show she was serious. The only problem was all her body wanted to do was break down into a heap on the floor and sob.

"You don't have to, Ava," Zach said. "You could stay here. We could figure this out together."

She shook her head. "We can't, Zach. It's too dangerous."

And that's when Zach held the letter in both his hands and held it closer to his face to read through the dim light. "'I've been madly, head over heels in love with you for years. Maybe since the moment I first laid eyes on you.'" He looked into her eyes then. "It's like you took the words right out of my head. This is all exactly how

I feel. And now, after everything, I don't know how I could bear to lose my best friend. But I don't know how I could bear to lose the love of my life too."

"I know," Ava managed to say. "But this is the only way. Maybe someday but…"

She picked up the bag she'd packed and tried to push past him, but Zach put his hand out to stop her.

"Let me go, Zach. It's the only way to save the two of you," she said, pulling out of his gentle grip and spinning around toward the door.

And was immediately blocked by a very large, very solid body.

An arm attached to said body reached up, and Ava readied herself for another fight, not knowing how much she had left in her to do so. But the arm kept reaching, not in her direction, but toward…the wall?

The lights flicked on, and Ava was momentarily blinded, blinking, wholly discombobulated. And then her vision adapted, and a familiar face came into view.

Zach didn't know who the hell this guy was, but he swore he would take him out if he laid one finger on Ava. He hadn't known he had it in him, but all the violence of the night seemed to be simmering right on the surface, and Zach was ready to punch the bushy, gray handlebar mustache right off the guy if he had to.

"George?" Ava said, confusion heavy in her eyes.

"Hey guys, am I interrupting something?" the older man said, with an expression on his face that was not at all subtle about the amusement he was getting out of the situation.

"George? What the hell are you doing here?" Ava

asked, looking like she was readying to punch him in the shoulder for scaring her like that.

The man—George—sauntered in without a care in the world and quietly shut the door before he sat on the couch, taking up more space than seemed possible on the large sofa.

"Well," George said, "I wanted to let you know we got him."

"What are you talking about?"

"We got the Crow."

What the hell was that supposed to mean, Zach wondered, but to be frank, George was kind of an intimidating man, and Zach didn't particularly think interrupting him was the best idea.

"What?" Ava asked, as if it were impossible to believe what George was saying. She moved to a chair near George and sat. "How are you even here?" She shook her head a little, as if trying to clear it.

"Well, it's a bit of a long story, and it kind of looks like you were getting ready to leave, so maybe I should leave it for another time."

The guy was starting to remind Zach of his annoying uncle Arthur, who loved the sound of his own voice and dragged his stories out just to get another few seconds of attention.

"George!" Ava said.

And that was all it took. George chuckled a little, but finally started explaining. "I have an old army buddy who's helped me out quite a bit over the years. In fact, he helped me set you up here in this charming little town."

Ava's eyebrows knit together in the most adorable way, as Zach moved to sit. He tried to be discreet about it, but hobbling around mostly on one leg tended to draw attention.

When everyone was settled, George went on. "I think you all may have had a run in or two with him."

Ava's eyes alighted with understanding. "The cop."

George nodded admiringly. "Officer Banyan, to be exact. He and I have kept in touch with one another all these years. In fact, he's been keeping an eye on you." He turned to Ava, his eyes twinkling.

"Is he okay?" Zach interrupted. "The last time I saw him, he looked kind of...dead."

"Luckily, not quite," George said. "When I didn't hear from him when I was supposed to, I got the hell out here and tracked his phone. Lost the signal a little way away from the acreage, but I eventually got to him. He was pretty loopy, but I called the ambulance out to that nice acreage in the forest and they're getting him right as rain. He's at the hospital now."

"Holy shit," Ava said. "And Justin?"

"Told ya," George said. "We got him."

Wait. The Crow is Justin? Realization flooded over Zach. "And you're Sparrow," he said, remembering what Chloe had repeated from her captor.

"Yes," Ava said absently, apparently still trying to wrap her head around everything. "So, it's over?"

"It's over," George said, putting his hand on her knee like a father might. "It's really over this time. They've got Justin in custody. I still don't know who he's working for, and we don't want to risk revealing your real identity, or the fact that Zach here," George continued, turning to acknowledge Zach, "and Chloe are involved, so the state authorities have agreed to work with us to keep all that quiet. But the charges of break and enter out at the acreage, as well as the attempted murder of Officer Banyan, should keep him behind bars for a very long time."

Ava opened her mouth to say something, but nothing came out. She shook her head again as if she still couldn't believe it.

Hope was building inside of Zach, but he was scared to say anything, afraid he might jinx…well, everything.

"Well," George said, clapping his hands together, almost as if washing them clean of the whole ordeal, "I'd better get over to the station. Make sure everything goes smoothly."

George bent down and kissed Ava on the top of the head. "See ya around, kid," he said, then turned to Zach and held his hand out.

Zach stood—after a bit of a struggle—and shook it. "Nice to meet you, sir," he said.

"Likewise," George said, with a nod of his head.

And with that, George sauntered away like he hadn't just delivered the kind of news that changed lives forever.

"What the hell was that?" Zach asked.

Ava blinked. "I think," she began, the words tentative. "I think it was George giving me my life back. Again."

"What do you mean 'again'?"

"He was the one who saved me from Justin the first time. Five years ago. I'd sent him a text, and he got to me, somehow found the strength to pull me out of a burning inferno."

"Jesus," Zach said, shaking his head at the idea Ava might have been through worse than any of them had gone through that day. "I'm sorry."

Ava shrugged. "But in the end, it brought me here."

Zach couldn't hold back any longer from asking the question his mind had been quite distractedly screaming at him for the past ten minutes. "So does this mean you can stay?"

Ava seemed to be thinking about it as he held his breath. He didn't know if he could take another letdown tonight. Or for the next half century or so.

"I think," she said, pausing once more to give it a final mulling. "I think I can," she told him, her eyes widening in delight like a kid at a carnival.

Zach finally saw the thing he now knew he'd been wishing for, for years. An understanding surging between them that the time for questioning was past, and in its place, a realization that they belonged to each other. He went to her, his leg not quite letting him forget he was hurt, but since his entire life had been stolen away and then given back to him in a matter of hours, he was not about to waste even a single second more.

Chapter 22

Zach knelt on his good leg in front of Ava's chair and leaned up for a kiss, and what else could Ava do but meet him halfway, her heart thrumming, her skin humming, and everything inside her tingling.

The kiss was slow, and maybe even a little questioning still, each of them asking, *are you sure?* Of course, neither of them had ever been so sure of anything in their lives.

Ava slipped her hands under the edge of his T-shirt and lifted it over his head, holding his gaze, trying not to wince at the pain zipping through her arm. Concern filled Zach's eyes and Ava hated that she was stopping the moment of intimacy, but his focus only turned to her injured arm, holding it so gently, so lovingly, then softly wisping the lightest of kisses along it.

The carefulness, the tenderness should have brought forth thoughts of sweetness. But knowing that this man, this beautiful, good, courageous man cared for her so wholly—cherished her—made it, oddly, the most seductive moment she'd ever known. Each almost imperceptible brush of his lips triggered sensations that hadn't been roused in years.

Maybe it was relief knowing the moment that had been building for years, maybe even from the first time she saw him that night on her front porch, beer in hand, and each moment after, had finally led them to meaning everything to each other. First as best friends and now to this…to their very own forever. Forever was not a concept Ava had allowed herself to think about, and even now it scared her, but as Zach made his way up her arm with his kisses, over her shoulder and to her neck, thoughts started to retract, becoming far away and unimportant.

Zach found her lips again just as he found the hem of her shirt, pulling it up and pausing for breath as he maneuvered her good arm out of it, then over her head, so careful when he slid it over the bandage on her other arm. He flung the shirt gently to the couch and turned back to her, just looking at her for a moment.

"Hey," he said, his voice husky and ragged.

"Hey," she said back, smiling and wholly content.

Over the years they'd built this thing where they checked in with each other, brought each other back to the moment when things started to get a little too stressful, a little too overwhelming, a little too…well, grumpy on Zach's end. Ava knew this was what they were doing now. Checking in. Coming back to the moment. Connecting.

All this time she'd been so afraid to lose Zach, but she realized it wasn't just Zach the man, it was their relationship. It was the reason they had never gone down this path before, the fear that things would change.

The moment lasted only a second before their lips met again, but it shoved away all the uncertainty and solidified that they were still going to be them—best friends. And now, obviously more, but still them. Ava felt something heavy lift from her.

Suddenly, she was so alive, so hungry for this man she loved more than she'd loved anything in her life, her hands exploring, moving across his skin. His lips drowning her in a desperate kiss before moving downward, kissing his way along as his hand fumbled behind to release her bra, his lips finding her breast, ravenously taking it into his mouth. Every nerve came alive, pulsing, thirsting for more. She couldn't get enough as he moved to the other side, his strong hands tight around her as he grazed, licked, and, in Ava's admittedly biased opinion, unabashedly thrilled his audience of one, her breath coming in gasps.

She fumbled for his button, his zipper, excruciatingly difficult with only one good hand and a need so urgent she thought she might die if she didn't get to him.

"Let me help," Zach said, grinning and regrettably moving away from her, leaning heavy on the arm of the chair as he mostly used only his good leg to stand.

What a pair they were, Ava thought, though she had to admit, she was absolutely going to enjoy this show while it lasted. Once balanced on one leg, Zach gingerly peeled his jeans partway down, the bandage stark white against his skin, though that was decidedly not where her attention landed given the rather impressive arousal situation going on.

He stopped halfway through the removing of his pants and Ava turned her attention back to his face, which was looking a bit more sheepish than you'd expect someone to be in that situation.

"What?" Ava asked, concern rising.

"I, uh, kinda need to sit down for this part," he said, kind of shrugging and hobbling over to the couch, flopping heavily and struggling to free himself of the particularly difficult and maddening jeans.

Ava tilted her head, a smile spreading across her face. "Works for me," she said, standing.

As she stood, she imagined she'd strip in an erotic, seductive way, but with her injured arm, she struggled with her own jeans, the button difficult but not impossible with the use of one good hand, then the actual removal of them being a kind of wriggling, hopping affair.

Sexy it was not, but at least they were both finally free of all obstacles.

"Quite a pair we make," Zach said, with a little chuckle.

Ava moved slowly toward him, gloriously exposed and feeling pretty damn sultry again all of a sudden. She moved close, pausing to allow him a good, long look, his eyes alight with appreciation, before she spoke. "The best pair, in my opinion," she said.

Zach smiled. "One might even say a perfect pair," he said, as he reached up for her, pulling her toward him.

Ava straddled her legs around his, careful of his injury, their lips meeting—urgently now, desperate to achieve their full pairing. As he lifted her and she slid onto him, she cried out in the relief of someone who'd waited and wanted for way too long.

Zach leaned his head back and closed his eyes, releasing a slow breath ending in a low groan like he'd been waiting just as long for this kind of relief. But there was so much more relief to be had as Ava began to move, slowly at first, then quickening as he rose to meet her in a rhythm so natural it was like they were made for each other. Zach found her breast with his mouth again and it was like a string that ran straight through her was pulled taut, the pressure building to unsustainable levels, and then he began to suck, ever so gently. Ava nearly whimpered with need, and as he thrust to meet that need, he sucked harder, the string stretching to the point of no return, and then finally, gloriously breaking as she erupted with a cry that sent Zach reeling over the edge too, surging to his own climax with a sexy, primal roar of a sound as he held her tight—protective, loving, like he was never letting her go.

And she hoped to hell he never would.

Epilogue

They decided a car accident was the best way to explain Zach's limp, Ava's messed-up arm, and the fact that Zach was missing a truck. Officer Banyan had been true to his word, only reporting what was necessary to put Justin in prison and keep him there for a very long while.

Ava and Zach made their debut as a couple two days later by taking a slow walk, hand in hand up Main Street, right through all the people from town who were packing up their booths and tents, the air filled with scents of a crisp fall breeze, some remnants of apple-scented goodies and a touch of sadness that it was all over for another year.

Everyone turned to stare, but not one gaze in the crowd had even the slightest hint of surprise. In fact, as the pair approached, there was more than one murmur of the word *finally* and quite a few knowing glances and approving nods.

When they reached The Other Apple Store, Maureen was waiting for them on the stoop.

"Thank you so much for keeping the place going," Ava said, as she hugged her friend.

"Of course," Maureen said. "We were so worried when you didn't show the other morning, but I figured the least I could do was man the store for a day. When we heard about the accident, I nearly fainted. I'm so sorry I didn't come looking for you or send help or something."

Even though they were bombarded with questions, Ava and Zach kept their answers to the onslaught of questions as vague as possible. Decided to go for a hike. Truck ran off the road. Took them a while to get help and make it back.

Keep it simple and boring, so fewer questions would be asked.

"What you did was exactly what I needed," Ava said, hugging her one more time.

"Well, would you look at that," Barney said, stopping his packing to raise a hand over his eyes to block the sun.

Someone let out a low whistle from a few stalls down and Miss Clara gasped. "Captain Applebottom!" she yelled, as she started running toward her prized chicken. "You've come back to me!"

Sure enough, as Ava gazed up the street, Captain Applebottom was strolling back on into town as if he didn't have a care in the world—safe, sound and pecking at the ground every few steps.

"Guess the little guy wasn't too keen on being the town's damn mascot," Zach said, eyes twinkling with newfound respect. "Now that is one smart bird."

And as Miss Clara scooped Captain Applebottom into her arms, the town resumed its packing.

So many people she'd come to know and love over

the years—Barney, who was already on Miss Clara's case for letting Captain Applebottom get loose in the first place, Donna Mae from the antique store, Jackson packing up his hardware sale, Annie, who was helping some of the others since her knitting had been washed out in the water tower incident, and so many others. People she tried not to let into her heart but who had wriggled their way in anyway.

She felt a warm hand take hers. Zach. The only best friend she'd ever had, and from across the street, Chloe running toward them, clearly with a plan on her mind.

"Can we get one last apple-cinnamon ice cream?" she asked Zach.

"Who? You and me?" Zach asked.

Chloe rolled her eyes. "Obviously not," she said. "Me and Emma. We want something for the walk to the park."

Zach chuckled and dug into his pocket for some money as Ava took a good, long look at her town.

At all the people milling around doing their thing, at Zach, who looked as content as she'd ever seen him, at Chloe rushing back toward Emma, and she realized, for the first time since she'd arrived in Ambrosia Falls, there was absolutely nothing hanging over her head. Nothing stopping her from letting the whole town fill her up. Nothing in the way of enjoying each single mundane, everyday moment. Nothing that could ever force her to leave.

Zach pulled her hand back into his like that was its new home now. "Well, thank goodness that's over," he said, in his signature grumpy way.

For all the quirks of the town and the people in it,

Ava realized with a grin, there was not a single thing she would change.

"Yup," she said, a smile spreading across her face. "And I absolutely can't wait till next year."

* * * * *